How to Bewitch an Earl

How to Bewitch an Earl

ALLY BROADFIELD

Entangled Publishing, LLC
2614 South Timberline Road
Suite 109
Fort Collins, CO 80525
Visit our website at www.entangledpublishing.com.

Scandalous is an imprint of Entangled Publishing, LLC.

Edited by Robin Haseltine
Cover Design by Heather Howland
Cover Art by Period Images

ISBN 978-1-68281-058-3

Manufactured in the United States of America

First Edition November 2015

To my dad, who convinced me that I could do anything if I was willing to put enough effort into it. Thank you for being my biggest fan despite the fact that you have no intention of ever reading a romance.

Prologue

The rain beat a steady tempo against the glass panes of the window as Catherine rushed up the cold, damp staircase to Edward's bedchamber. She pulled her shawl more tightly about her shoulders and increased her pace. She was running late. As usual.

"I'm sorry I'm late, darling."

"I don't mind, Mama. It means I get to stay awake longer. And I'm used to you being late."

She squeezed onto the bed next to him and kissed his forehead. "Which story would you like me to tell tonight?"

He pretended to think about it, then blurted out, "The one about the tiara."

Of course. He requested that story every night, regardless of whether it was her or Nick putting him to bed.

Leaning close, she whispered, "Hidden somewhere in this house is a diamond tiara once owned by Empress Elizabeth of Russia."

He bounced up and down on the bed. "You forgot to say 'Empress of all the Russias.'"

She tweaked his nose. "My apologies for leaving off that very important detail." His eyelids drooped. She pulled him tight against her side and leaned back against the pillows.

"Now where was I? Oh yes, the tiara is located somewhere in this house, but because an evil cousin sold all of the furniture and didn't take good care of Walsley Manor, we weren't able to locate it."

"And it has never been found."

She nodded. "That is correct. The tiara is still here in this house, waiting for someone to find it."

He waved both hands. "Me!"

"When you are older we will give you the journal so you can solve the clues."

He nodded. "And find the tiara."

She touched the tip of her finger to his nose. "Perhaps, but first you will need to investigate to discover where it is."

"I will use Great-Grandmother's journal to find it."

"Right now the journal is safe in your father's library, but when you are grown, we will let you read the journal and find the clues to the location of the tiara."

"I will find the tiara." She smiled at his confidence as he snuggled down under the covers and closed his eyes.

She kissed him and pulled up the coverlet. "Pleasant dreams, darling." As she moved into the corridor, she spotted a star outside the window and wished for Edward to have happy dreams about discovering lost family treasures.

Chapter One

LONDON, ENGLAND
JUNE 1846

Edward Adair, the Earl of Kenworth and heir to the Duke of Boulstridge, briefly considered entering the house through a window. After all, using a knife to open locks was one of the more practical skills his mother had taught him, though perhaps it wasn't the best idea when he was at least two sheets to the wind. What he really needed to do was secure lodgings of his own so he could come and go as he pleased without censure.

In any case, Phillips had waited up for him, so attempting to sneak in was out of the question.

"Good morning, my lord." Phillips bowed. "The duke and duchess await your presence in the library."

Of course they did. Because a good, stern lecture would surely fix all that ailed him. He wandered down the corridor and entered the library. Though a fire burned merrily in the hearth, there was a decided lack of warmth in the room.

His father stood and shot him a deep scowl before opening his mouth to speak, but Mother cut him off, bless her.

"Edward, we are concerned about you. Your only pursuits seem to be drinking and carousing with your friends, and occasionally pouring over the clues in the journal."

He crossed his arms. "Mother, you of all people should understand my dedication to solving the mystery."

She approached him and placed her palm against his cheek. "Darling, you know I'm not asking you to give up the search altogether. No one wants to find the tiara more than I do, but you cannot allow the mystery to devour you. It should not be an all-consuming occupation for you."

As if he had anything else to occupy his time, so long as his father refused to cede any responsibility to him.

"It's not as if I'm off gambling away my inheritance or consorting with prostitutes."

His father clenched his jaw but didn't speak, likely assuming his steely expression would quell Edward.

"You must find a way to search while also maintaining other pursuits," Mother said.

"Such as?"

His father stepped forward. "Managing your estates."

He held back a belch and wished he had taken advantage of the opportunity to sneak in through a window. "I wasn't aware that my estates were in disarray."

"Of course they are not, no thanks to you. Though we have excellent staff in place, it is still necessary for you to be involved, to learn how to handle these issues yourself, without me watching over your shoulder."

Many possible responses flashed through his mind, but it would do no good to voice any of them. His father maintained iron control over everything within his dukedom, so anything Edward did was irrelevant, as his father had the final say.

He took a step toward his father and mirrored his unyielding stance. "Until you are willing to allow me to make decisions on my own without your approval, there is little point in my participation."

His father's eyes flashed, but Mother stepped between them and placed her hand on his arm before he could respond.

"Our point is, you need to engage in activities other than those that have been occupying all of your time of late. You could travel, explore antiquities," Mother added. "You used to enjoy the study of other cultures."

As if Mother hadn't spoken at all, his father took another step toward him and said, "You could also behave like a responsible gentleman who deserves to inherit a dukedom and an enormous fortune." He paused and met Edward's eyes. "You have missed several parliamentary sessions. The purpose of getting you a seat in the House of Commons was to help prepare you to assume your position in the House of Lords when I am gone. You need to take your responsibilities seriously."

Though his accusation was unfounded, as Edward had only missed a handful of meetings during the prior session, there was no point in arguing with him.

"It's not enough to just attend sessions. You need to get involved, take the lead on an issue or introduce a new law. Your only accomplishment of late has been to have your name linked to an opera singer. I cannot disinherit you, but I can choose to remove all of the unentailed properties from your inheritance and, if your behavior doesn't change immediately, I shall."

So he intended to force Edward to bend to his will.

Mother shot him a stern look then turned back to Edward. "Darling, we simply feel that it is time for you to find some other worthy pursuit." She turned and strode to the other side of the library. "I…we think that it is time for you to settle down. Toward that end, we are arranging a house party at Walsley Manor in a fortnight. I've already made a list of eligible ladies for you to consider, and of course you may invite some of your own friends."

He narrowly refrained from rolling his eyes. "What are you hoping the end result of this party will be?"

Mother smiled. "For you to find a wife, of course. Once you find the right woman, settling down won't seem like such a hardship."

He highly doubted that.

Father narrowed his eyes at Edward. "And if you don't choose someone, you will be cut off. You may find a way to support yourself until such a time as I die and you can take control of the entailed properties. But don't forget, Walsley is not entailed, and as such, I do not have to leave it to you." He turned and stormed from the room.

Edward rubbed his forehead. Though it was sometimes difficult to discern, after a lifetime of living with the man, he knew his father acted out of love. But he made it damned difficult to remember when his approach was always to bully and cajole to force his position. There was some merit to his father's concerns, but until he gave Edward at least a modicum of responsibility for something, it was pointless for him to become more involved.

"Has he ever considered that it is his lack of confidence in me that prevents me from taking an active interest in managing our properties? I might be more proactive if he deemed me trustworthy."

"Darling." Mother clasped his hand. "He is simply concerned for your welfare. I will speak with him about allowing you to manage one of the smaller estates on your own. In the meantime, though we will not force you to marry, you do need to settle down and find some sort of worthwhile pursuit in addition to our quest for the tiara."

"I think you are overly optimistic about the results of this house party."

She smiled. "Your father is not an ogre. He simply wishes to see you settled, but even he does not wish for you to make a foolish match. We ask only that you carefully consider the merit of the ladies you meet at the party, and also put more thought into what you wish to make of your life."

Even in his inebriated state, he could see that their perspective was valid, but he wasn't in any condition to do something about it. The glow of the sun rising filtered around the curtains in the east-facing windows.

Mother took his arm and towed him toward the door. "Come, we must get some rest. Make a list of your friends, and especially any ladies who've caught your eye, so I can include them in the invitations."

He nodded. Though his parents were both astute at avoiding those families who were only interested in the advantage they would gain by marrying their daughter off to a future duke, they seemed desperate enough to see him married that they might relax their normal standards. Inviting a dozen or so of his chums would help deflect some of the attention he was sure to receive, especially from the meddling mamas of the girls who would attend.

"We only want what's best for you." She kissed him on the cheek and rushed up the staircase.

If only he could be certain what was best for himself.

Chapter Two

Derbyshire, England
July 1846

Isabella Winthrop glanced around her bedchamber one last time, but there was nothing else for her to do. Everything was clean, folded, and where it belonged. Lady Concord had retired earlier, leaving Isa, her paid companion, with nothing to do. Going to bed before the sun went down would never do, as she had enough difficulty falling asleep when it was dark outside.

The house party did not begin for another week, so they were currently the only guests at Walsley Manor. In fact, Lord Kenworth, in whose honor the party was being held, wasn't even in residence. Lady Concord had been a close friend of Her Grace's mother, and as such, was welcome to arrive a bit early. However, it left Isa with nothing to occupy her time in the evenings. Perhaps she could ask to visit the library and borrow a book. It wasn't an unusual request and required no special effort on behalf of anyone in the household.

Isa exited into the corridor and descended the staircase. Ever since she had accepted her position as a companion, she had worked hard to be as unnoticeable as possible. Plain clothing and simple hairstyles rendered her nearly invisible within the homes of the nobility, who were well practiced at ignoring the servants.

She glanced at the family portraits as she went down the staircase. The Duke of Boulstridge was a handsome man, as was his son.

Turning her head at the last possible second before she reached the final stair, she narrowly avoided a collision with the duchess.

"Miss Winthrop." She placed a hand on Isa's shoulder. "My apologies for nearly running you off the stair. You and Lady Concord have been such self-sufficient guests that I had almost forgotten you were here."

"Thank you, Your Grace, but I'm afraid the fault is mine. I was focused on the portraits and wasn't paying attention to where I was going."

The duchess raised a brow. "Yes, His Grace is a handsome man, but I imagine you would be more interested in my son."

Her stomach clenched. "Oh no, Your Grace. I would never aspire to…that is…assume that—"

"Miss Winthrop, would you care to join me for a cup of tea?"

Surprised by her abrupt invitation, she blurted out, "I would be delighted, Your Grace."

"Excellent. Follow me." She turned and strode back down the corridor she had come from and into a cozy sitting room that Isa hadn't realized existed. Not that she had been randomly exploring the house on her own. Not when her position hung on her ability to remain unnoticed. Though Isa had never met him, Lord Kenworth had attended Eton with her brother, and it would ruin everything if he were to discover her true identity.

The duchess waved toward a chair and rang the bell. "Please, make yourself comfortable." Isa sat, and one of Her Grace's small dogs that followed her everywhere jumped up to join her. Her heart tightened. She scratched behind his ears and laughed as he rolled over onto his back so Isa could scratch his stomach. The little mixed breed reminded her of her own dog, which she had had to leave with George when she left to take up her position as Lady Concord's companion.

Isa glanced around the room as the duchess spoke to a maid. This had to be her private sitting room, because it was rather disorganized. Fabric swatches were piled on one side table, and books with various items sticking out of them, that she supposed were used to mark pages, littered nearly every available surface.

Once the maid left, the duchess sat across from her on a well-cushioned chaise longue. "My apologies for the clutter in here, but it is my private chamber, and I do not allow anyone else to clean it. I cannot find anything if someone else organizes it." She shot her a smile and continued. "His Grace has long since stopped entering the room, as the disarray drives him to distraction. I suspect that is why in this excessively large house, I am only allowed this one chamber for my own. His Grace would surely have an apoplexy if he had to view multiple rooms in such disorder."

Isa bit back a smile. By all accounts, theirs was a love match. Because Lady Concord had been a close friend of Her Grace's mother, Isa had not received any of the usual gossip from her. "I understand completely. Before Lady Concord hired me, I was infamous for accumulating all manner of items. My bedchamber back home was always a wreck, and I refused to allow the maids to enter my room. My brother called me a little piglet when we were younger."

Her Grace tilted her head to the side for a moment and hesitated before returning Isa's smile. A lightning bolt seared her stomach. She had revealed too much. Unless the family had recently fallen on hard times, paid companions didn't generally grow up in a situation that included a family with several servants.

A knock heralded the arrival of their tea, and they were silent as the maid set everything out.

"Let us be informal." Her Grace poured the tea, and they each prepared their own cups. Noticing the dog on Isa's lap, she said, "Oh dear, is Biscuit bothering you?"

"Oh, no, Your Grace. I am quite fond of dogs. He reminds me of my own dog that I had to leave behind with my brother when I moved to Lady Concord's house.

The duchess smiled. "I am glad to hear that you are so fond of dogs. I'm always suspicious of people who are not." She set her cup on the table. "I'm not sure how much you've heard about me. Are you familiar with my background?"

Isa thought back to what Lady Concord had shared with her and shook her head. "No, Your Grace. Lady Concord has often mentioned your mother as a dear friend, but that is the extent of my knowledge."

"That is what I thought. Well, then you must let me tell

you my story. I'm afraid it is a bit long and convoluted, but hopefully you will not find it boring."

Isa nodded, eager to hear what she would say.

"Lady Concord knows a bit of our history. You see, my mother grew up in this house. "Isa narrowed her eyes. "I don't understand. I thought the house belonged to His Grace."

"He likes people to think that, and he did own it at one time, but the house now belongs to me. Anyway, long before His Grace purchased the manor, my family owned the property. My grandfather died, and the title passed on to his cousin, so my mother and grandmother were forced to leave the house. They embarked on a long voyage to America to live with a distant cousin in Charleston. But they never made it that far."

"Oh my. I beg your pardon, Your Grace, but I feel as if I am reading a novel." Isa bit her lip. She was so intrigued by the story that she had overstepped her bounds. Again.

The duchess laughed, startling Biscuit out of his deep sleep. Isa stroked his side, and he soon relaxed.

"It does sound like the worst sort of penny fiction, does it not? And it will soon become even more convoluted."

She took a sip of tea before continuing. "My grandmother died during the ocean crossing, leaving my mother all alone. But luckily my father rescued her, and they live happily in the Bahamas and New Orleans, where his shipping business is located. Some still suspect him of being a pirate, an impression which he does not attempt to correct."

"Oh, my. How remarkable that His Grace was the owner of your former family home."

Her face colored. "Yes, well, it's not that remarkable. We met for the first time when I broke into the house to search for a family heirloom."

Isa bit her lip to prevent herself from voicing her wayward thoughts.

"I did attempt to behave properly at first. Suffice it to say, His Grace acted like a boar when I called on him and refused to see me, so I took matters into my own hands." She glanced up and smiled. "It did work out rather well for me in the end."

"I should think so." Perhaps there was some hope for Isa to find a happy ending of her own.

The duchess fiddled with her tea for a moment. "In any case, I wanted you to know my background. I am not of noble blood, and in fact there are many here who believe me to be the daughter of a pirate. Of course, none of them would dare say so in front of His Grace."

She took Isa's hand. "I am very inarticulate this evening, but what I am trying to say is that it is not necessary for you to be demure. Despite your best intentions to remain unnoticed, I recognized you immediately as a kindred spirit. I hope that sharing my own background with you will allow you to be more comfortable with me."

"Thank you, Your Grace." For one wild moment, she considered telling the duchess her story. But she could not risk it. Not until George was able to get out of debt. Perhaps someday she would be able to take her rightful place in society, but not yet.

"I very much appreciate you sharing your story with me. I shall remain hopeful that one day I might find a happy ending of my own." Not wanting to sound ungrateful for her position with Lady Concord, she added, "Of course, it's not as if working for Lady Concord is a burden. She is a kind and generous lady."

"Of course, my dear." She patted Isa's hand. "Do you by chance enjoy reading?"

"Yes, very much so."

"I thought as much, since you keep glancing at my books. Then I need to show you the library. You may go there at any time and read anything you choose." She drained her teacup and stood. "Are you ready?"

Isa nodded and stood. She wasn't at all surprised when Biscuit followed her down the corridor and into the most fantastic library she had ever seen in a private home. It wasn't just that it was enormous with rows and rows of books, but it was filled with large, cushioned furniture that one could curl up in, and a gargantuan fireplace that kept the room cozy and provided enough light to make lamps unnecessary, even after the sun set.

The duchess swept her arm toward the nearest shelves. "There are books on nearly every subject you can imagine, especially with respect to science and history. The novels are over on the far wall."

The number of books nearly overwhelmed her. Isa was giddy with the possibilities. Lady Concord enjoyed being read to, but it took them weeks to get through even one novel. She ran her hand down the spine of *Don Quixote*, which was one of her favorites, then came upon all of Jane Austen's works, which she had read many times.

Then she found it. *The Count of Monte Cristo.* It was on the list she had made to keep track of the books she read with Lady Concord, but she could not pass up the chance to read it now. Though Lady Concord was very generous, reading aloud to her at such a slow pace didn't completely fulfill Isa's desire to escape into other worlds. After gently removing it from the shelf, she ran her hand over the cover.

The duchess moved to stand next to her. "You have not read it yet?"

Isa shook her head.

"Then you must take it. We also have *The Three Musketeers* if you're interested." She slid it from the shelf and handed it to Isa. "Don't be shy. You may take as many books as you want up to your chamber. I'm not sure if any of the ladies we've invited to the party are avid readers, but since you arrived first, you shall get the first selection."

Isa bit her lower lip. They had long since sold off the contents of the library at home, not to mention most of the furnishings, so George could complete necessary repairs to the house.

"Thank you, Your Grace. I cannot imagine a pleasure more acute than spending hours lost in a story." She was very lucky to have an employer who not only shared her love of books but also gave her ample free time to read on her own.

"Take as many as you like and enjoy yourself." She yawned. "Now if you'll excuse me, it is past time for me to retire. If I wait much longer, His Grace will come looking for me."

"Good night," Isa said as the duchess swept from the room. Though she had made it clear that Isa could take as many books as she liked, she didn't wish to deprive the other guests, so she selected a few of her old favorites as well, including *Ivanhoe* and *Oliver Twist*, which Lady Concord had grown bored with so they never finished. Four books ought to be enough to keep her busy for the duration of the house party, but she took one last look to see if there were any other novels she couldn't pass by.

Strange. A book with no writing or defining marks on the outside was nearly hidden between *The Ugly Duckling* and *A Christmas Carol.* After running her hand down the smooth spine, she gently pulled it from the shelf. The leather was soft and worn in several places. She marshaled the courage to take a glance inside and found that it was a journal or diary of some sort.

She took a deep breath and let it out slowly. It wasn't right for her to read someone's diary. Surely it had been left here by accident. She hazarded a glance at the first page. It was simply an account of the dinner the author had planned for that evening, which led Isa to believe the journal belonged to a lady. After skimming through more than a third of the book, she came across a date. A house party that was held at Walsley in June of 1721. The journal must have belonged to one of Her Grace's ancestors, perhaps a great-aunt or great-grandmother.

No, it was wrong of her to read the journal, even if the author was long gone. Isa placed it back on the shelf and turned toward her stack of books, then stopped.

Her Grace had made it clear that Isa was welcome to read anything she wanted from the library, and if Her Grace had wished for it to remain private, surely she wouldn't have left it in the library for anyone to discover. Removing it from the shelf once again, she decided it wouldn't do any harm to read a bit more. She had always been fascinated by history, and how better to learn than through a personal account of the times.

Before delving into the journal, she settled onto the

settee and tucked a pillow behind her back to make herself comfortable. As an afterthought, she slipped off her half boots and lifted her feet onto the large piece of furniture. Biscuit immediately jumped up and curled himself against her legs. Skimming the pages about household accounts and gardening allowed her to get through another third of the book quickly. As she turned another page, the words leaped out at her.

"Not only has Walsley discovered the identity of my beau, but he is demanding that I give him the tiara. He plans to sell it, but I will never surrender it to him. It has been hidden."

Isa sat up straight. Tiara? Her beau? The duchess was correct that her family story read like a penny novel. She skimmed the next page and several more after that, until she reached a section that contained a clue as to where she had hidden the tiara.

"Begin where warmth abounds. Very close, yet worlds away, it is no place for the meek."

Isa repeated the words to herself. An oven? The fireplace? Glancing toward the fireplace in the library, which needed to be stoked, she noted the painting hanging above it. Could the clue refer to a painting? To the painting that hung above the fireplace? No. Upon closer inspection, the painting was of the current Duke and Duchess of Boulstridge. But surely another painting had once hung in that position.

Isa stood and stretched. She wished the duchess were still awake, as she wasn't sure she could sleep until she knew if the tiara had ever been found. Plunking herself back on the settee, she continued to read, searching for more clues. The room began to cool, and she pulled the blanket over her. As her eyelids grew heavier, she decided she ought to go to bed so she could get some sleep before Lady Concord needed her. She would just read one more page. The words began to blur, and she let her eyes flutter closed. It wouldn't hurt to rest for just a few moments before heading to her bedchamber.

Chapter Three

Edward ought to have timed his arrival better. Or perhaps he ought to have left London earlier. Though he certainly did not need someone to look after him, it might be a bit of a surprise to the household when he appeared in the morning. In fact, the barest of pink light had begun to peek over the eastern horizon. Morning was nearly upon them, and he hadn't slept at all. Perhaps he would delay his appearance until afternoon. A bit of sleep would do him some good, and neither he nor those who were invited to attend the house party were expected for several days.

Not wanting to wake any of the servants, he tiptoed past the library before remembering that Mother had written to let him know that she had obtained the full translation of *The Count of Monte Cristo*. After retracing his steps, he placed his palm against the unlatched door and gently pushed it open, then stopped as if he had run into a wall.

Someone was asleep on the settee. Someone young and

female. Someone with whom he was not acquainted.

As her breath whispered in and out, he realized there was an immediate intimacy in watching another person sleep. Something stirred inside him. She wasn't necessarily conventionally beautiful. Her light brown hair was rather ordinary in color, though the flickering fire revealed strands of both red and amber, and her mouth was wider and her lips fuller than normal. They were the sort of lips that were meant to be kissed, to feel trailing along one's—

Good grief. So she was intriguing. *But who was she?* The guests for the house party weren't set to arrive for another week. He took a step closer, and Biscuit trotted over to greet him. He bent down to give him a pat. Wait. *What was she holding?* He inched closer. Blood surged past his temples. It was the journal. He towered over her, waiting for the weight of his ire to wake her.

The woman's lids popped open within seconds, and she focused on him immediately, her eyes wide with…terror?

"How dare you," he practically shouted.

To her credit, she did not panic. After rubbing her eyes and refocusing her gaze on him, she calmly said, "I beg your pardon?"

He crossed his arms. "Who are you, and what are you doing in my library?"

"I could ask you the same question. Well, except for the library, which is most certainly not mine." She stood and stretched, arching her back in a most tantalizing fashion before continuing. "But it's not your library, either." She looked him up and down. "Who are you?"

He forced his gaze away from her breasts, which were more exposed than she probably realized, as her gown had slipped off one shoulder. Perhaps he ought to have told her, but the view was quite appealing. He shook his head and went back to the matter at hand. "I am Lord Kenworth. Who are you?"

"Oh, dear. I am no one of consequence." She glanced around the settee then continued. "The duchess gave me full access to the library last night, and I'm afraid I must have fallen asleep." She stood and picked up a stack of novels and moved to pass him. "If you'll excuse me, I must go tend to Lady Concord."

He sidestepped to block her exit and noted that one of the books she had chosen was the first volume of *The Count of Monte Cristo*. "Just a moment, if you please. What are you doing with that journal?"

"Oh." She turned back and lifted it from the cushion. "I found it between two of the novels on the shelf. It was quite diverting and—"

Ire swirled through his stomach. He crossed his arms. "Are you a simpleton?"

She opened her mouth to respond, but he cut her off.

"You don't look like one, but you must be to think that you can waltz into someone else's library and delve into a private journal with no compunction whatsoever."

She lifted her chin. "Now wait just a moment." She set the books down and crossed her arms over her chest. "I will thank you not to insult me. I was invited by the Duchess of Boulstridge to read anything I liked from the shelves of *her* library."

"Yes, well, *my* mother can sometimes be overly accommodating to our guests, but that hardly exonerates you."

"She was very specific that I...your mother?"

"Yes." He raised his brows and let that sink in for a moment. "In any case, you ought to have known that it was a private family journal and should have had the decency to refrain from reading it."

"It is more than a century old. Who am I hurting by reading it? And why is it in the library if it is meant to be kept private?"

"I…that is…" He completely lost his train of thought as rapid footsteps sounded in the corridor.

His mother swept through the open door. "Good morning, darling. I wasn't expecting you so soon." She leaned in and kissed his cheek then turned to their unwelcome guest. "Isabella, did you spent the night in my library?" She laughed.

"I'm afraid so, Your Grace." She glanced at Edward before continuing. "Apparently my presence here has caused offense. I am sorry if I overstepped my bounds." She ducked her head and moved toward the door with Biscuit trailing behind her. "I beg your pardon, Your Grace."

"Wait, Isabella. I don't understand." She turned on him. "What have you done?"

"Mother, I caught her reading the journal."

"And?"

"And it is an inexcusable breach of etiquette."

"An 'inexcusable breach of etiquette'? Since when did you become a judge of appropriate behavior?"

The wretched girl, apparently called Isabella, slapped a hand over her mouth, but it wasn't enough to quell her laughter.

"I am sorry my son was so rude to you." She glanced at his face. "Though it is no excuse, he appears to have traveled all night and is likely a bit out of sorts. If it helps, the Boulstridge men never seem to make a good first impression. I wanted to strangle His Grace the day we first met, and Edward is very much like his father."

Edward sighed. He wasn't the one behaving inappropriately.

"It is no matter, Your Grace." She shot him a side-eyed look then said, "If you don't mind me asking, was the tiara ever found?"

"No." Mother walked over to the interloper. "How much of the journal did you read?"

"I fell asleep somewhere after the riddle was revealed."

"Ah, but there is more than one riddle. Perhaps you should read the rest of the journal."

Edward took a step forward. "Absolutely not. Mother, what are you thinking?"

She narrowed her eyes at him. "That having another person read the clues, someone who doesn't have a stake in the matter, might be helpful to us."

"No, I must insist—"

The girl stepped forward. "Do not worry, my lord. I can see that I am not wanted here, and in any case, my duty is to Lady Concord, who is likely even now wondering where I am." She curtsied to his mother. "Your Grace, thank you for allowing me to explore your library. It has been a pleasure." She simply glared at him and exited the room without addressing him. Biscuit glanced at Edward, then made his decision and sped out of the room after her.

"Well, you've certainly made an excellent first impression on Miss Winthrop."

"I don't give a fig what impression that woman has of me. She is very bold for a servant, for heaven's sake."

"Darling, she is not a servant. She is Lady Concord's companion."

"That's barely a step up from a servant."

"And I am merely the daughter of a pirate."

"Grandfather is not a pirate."

She tapped her foot in a most annoying manner. "You do remember how your father and I first met, don't you?"

"Of course, but it's not the same."

"That is true. Miss Winthrop had my permission to read anything she wanted from the library, whereas I broke in with the intention of stealing something."

He paced over to the window. "Do you not find her terribly presumptuous to have read what was clearly a private family journal?"

"As she said, it was written more than a century ago. What harm could it do to have her read it?"

"You mean aside from allowing a presumably innocent girl to read inappropriate passages?"

"I read them when I was her age, and I managed to survive the experience."

He bit back a smile. "You're different. You've always been…unconventional."

"Perhaps Miss Winthrop is as well."

He wasn't so sure about that, though she was rather confident and bold for someone in her position. "That remains to be seen. What if she goes running off to her employer, complaining of inappropriate reading material?"

"I believe Lady Concord would be most pleased if Isabella read the journal aloud to her."

"Mother." He clenched his jaw. "It's not as if she is a candidate for marriage. Why involve her in our family mystery?"

"Perhaps because she is not. You've made certain that she will have no regard for you, so she will be free to focus on finding the tiara, rather than on chasing after you as all of the other young ladies will be doing."

He hadn't considered that. He would undoubtedly be spending most of his time avoiding the eligible young ladies his parents threw at him. As long as he didn't have to interact with the brazen chit, he supposed it wouldn't hurt to have someone with a fresh perspective read the journal. Besides, he would enjoy it in the end when she had no more luck than any of his family had in locating the tiara.

Chapter Four

What a presumptuous, odious, loathsome, unpleasant man. The duchess was so kind. Isa had no idea how her son had managed to turn out so horribly. George had also spoken well of him, but he must have changed for the worse once he left school. However, she needed to remember herself. She'd always had a quick temper, but she would do well to be more careful here at Walsley, lest she create suspicion about her background. No one in a position of service spoke to members of the nobility the way she had spoken to Lord Kenworth.

After taking the stairs two at a time to burn off some of her fury, she had made it nearly all the way to her bedchamber before she realized that she had left her books in the library. Since she had no desire to see Lord Kenworth again, she would wait to fetch them.

Isa bathed and quickly changed into a fresh gown then stopped to check on Lady Concord, but she wasn't in her chamber. She must have gone down to breakfast already. Over the past few months, she had begun to retire earlier at night and rise earlier in the mornings.

While rushing down the corridor, she nearly collided with Louisa, the daughter of the duke and duchess, whom she'd met the previous day.

"Good morning," Louisa said cheerfully. "I see Biscuit has taken a liking to you." He flipped onto his back and she bent and rubbed his stomach. "Did you sleep well?"

Isa shook her head. "I'm afraid not, but it is my own fault, as I fell asleep on the settee in the library." She refrained from telling Louisa that her horrid brother was the one who had woken her.

"Oh? What were you reading that kept you so occupied?"

"Nothing special." Though the duchess certainly didn't seem to mind her reading the journal, she didn't want to risk alienating any other members of the family after Lord Kenworth's reaction. "I am looking forward to reading *The Count of Monte Cristo*. I may read it aloud to Lady Concord if she is amenable."

"Perhaps we could take turns reading. I believe Mother is the only one of us who has already read it. We can start this afternoon."

Isa shook her head. "Don't be silly. I will choose something else to read so you can have it to yourself."

"Nonsense. It will be so much fun to read it together. My brother is especially entertaining when reading aloud. I'm certain I can convince him to join us once he arrives."

Isa found it very difficult to imagine that. "If you're speaking of Lord Kenworth, he arrived early this morning, but I'm not sure he'd be amenable to having me join in the fun."

Her brows lowered. "What makes you think that?"

Isa decided she might as well tell Louisa that she had been reading the journal. She was bound to find out anyway. "I stumbled upon the family journal, and he took exception to my reading it."

"Yes, of all of us, he is the most obsessed with finding the tiara. Even more so than Mama." She reached for Isa's hand. "Don't let him bother you. He can be a grump, but he's really quite wonderful once you get to know him."

Isa snorted, and they both laughed.

"You'll see." Louisa squeezed her hand.

Isa listened contentedly as Louisa read the second chapter. Following breakfast, the duchess had given them a tour of the rose gardens, and after freshening up, they agreed to meet in the library for tea and to read *The Count of Monte Cristo*. Lady Concord was not a strict employer. In fact, she really didn't need a companion at all, but she had been a close friend of Isa's mother and had offered her the position when circumstances began to deteriorate at home. Such an undemanding employer was difficult to come by, and Isa knew she was lucky. There were far worse positions to be in.

Isa stiffened as footsteps sounded in the corridor. Lord Kenworth poked his head through the doorway. Louisa used her finger to hold her place and glanced up at him.

"Edward. You must take over the reading."

He greeted Lady Concord and nodded to Isa then glanced at the book. "But I haven't read it yet and am not familiar with the beginning."

His sister made a *tsk*ing sound. "That is no matter. I can summarize for you. Edmond arrives home to France after having acted as captain of his ship when the original captain dies. He finds out that his father has not fared well in his absence, and we discover that his neighbor and the supercargo from the ship are plotting against him."

"Don't forget that he met Napoleon on his way back to France," Isa added.

Lord Kenworth swung around to glare at her, as if he hadn't remembered her presence until she had spoken. Perhaps due to his contrary nature, Isa was dismayed to find that he was much more handsome than she had remembered. Of course, his arrogant stance and commanding personality meant that he knew it, which was not at all attractive. But she could not deny that his eyes were startlingly green, and his chiseled profile put her in mind of a statue of Zeus she had once admired at the British Museum. A glance at the duchess confirmed that the vivid color of his eyes had come from her, but there was no doubt that his dark hair, wide shoulders, and height, not to mention his confident bearing, had come from the duke.

Louisa's eyes narrowed as she glanced back and forth between them before speaking. "Yes, I suspect that might become important later on." She thrust the book toward her brother. "Now you read."

His mouth lifted at one corner. "Very well. If you insist."

Her stomach fluttered, and she grumpily wondered if he had perfected that half smile in front of his mirror. While scooting to the side to make room for Louisa to sit, Isa shifted so she could watch him. His expressions changed with each character he read. When he wasn't chastising her, the deep tones of his voice were quite pleasant, melodious even. Louisa had been correct. He was an accomplished actor, but was there more to him? Or was everything he did an affectation?

Needing to halt her wayward thoughts, she stroked Biscuit and closed her eyes for a moment. Lord Kenworth was someone she might have been attracted to if they had met in her previous life. If they had met as equals. Of course, she had no interest in a man who looked down upon others and judged them by their station in life rather than their merit, but she suspected there were many more facets to his personality hidden behind that arrogant facade.

In any case, she wanted to hear the story, so she forced herself to focus on Lord Kenworth's words rather than him. Fernand was attempting to persuade Mercedes to marry him, but she loved Edmond and was quite firm in her reply.

"I have answered you a hundred times, Fernand, and really you must be very stupid to ask me again."

Biting back a giggle at his high-pitched voice, Isa wished she had had the nerve to speak to Lord Kenworth that candidly last night. He could certainly benefit from being put in his place at regular intervals. She allowed herself to be drawn back into the story when Edmond arrived to claim Mercedes.

"Ah," exclaimed the young girl, blushing with delight, and fairly leaping in excess of love, "you see he has not forgotten me, for here he is!" And rushing towards the door, she opened it, saying, "Here, Edmond, here I am!"

With the similarity between their names, Isa couldn't help but imagine, for just a moment, that it was Lord

Kenworth who had returned and was seeking her out. She allowed herself a moment to enjoy the silky depth of his voice, the way he conveyed the magnitude of Mercedes's love through his lilting tone, which swept over her like a caress. Louisa had been correct that her brother was an exceptional storyteller, but she also thought that made him an excellent actor as well. She would keep her guard around him.

When they reached the end of chapter three, which left them without resolution and therefore wanting more, Her Grace rose from her chair.

"I think this is a good place to stop for today. Thank you, Isabella, for joining in the reading. Our family tends to fight for that privilege, so we welcome your calming influence." The duchess escorted Lady Concord to her chamber, leaving Isa to gather her things and straighten up the settee. She moved Biscuit to the floor and folded the blanket, then moved the pillows back to their original arrangement. As she worked, she attempted to ignore the weight of Lord Kenworth's burning stare.

"We have servants for that sort of thing, you know."

She nodded. "Yes, and I am one of them. Well, Lady Concord's, that is."

"A companion is not the same as a servant."

"It might as well be."

He studied her for an uncomfortable moment, then cleared his throat. "My mother has convinced me that it is in our best interest to have someone disengaged from the search read the journal."

Isa stopped fussing with the pillows and met his eyes. "You don't look convinced."

"Consider me skeptical but willing to give it a try."

She bit back a grin. That was likely as conciliatory as he would get.

He thrust the journal at her. "Here. Take it before I change my mind."

"My lord, what an honor it is to receive your vote of confidence." At least he had the temerity to look sheepish.

"Yes, well, it's not as if any of us have had luck solving the riddle."

"Her Grace stated that there was more than one riddle in the journal. Have you had luck in solving any of them?"

He sighed. "No. It would seem that they must be solved in order, so until we solve the first riddle, we have no hope of deciphering the others."

Isa opened the journal and gently flipped the pages until she found the first riddle.

"Begin where warmth abounds. Very close, yet worlds away, it is no place for the meek."

"I had assumed the first riddle was referring to a painting that had hung over the fireplace."

His eyes narrowed. "Yes, that is what we determined as well."

She tilted her head toward the existing painting. "But that is clearly not the painting we are looking for. Have you searched for it?"

"Extensively. I don't know how much my mother told you about the house, but it had been stripped of its contents and left in disrepair before my father bought it."

"So we know for certain that it is no longer in the house." She strode over to the window and glanced at the gently falling rain. "I don't suppose you have a painting of the tiara?"

He moved to stand next to her, the heat from him causing her to shiver. "No, but when you read further in the journal, you'll find that rumors abounded about its provenance."

She turned to face him, then took a step back. He was unnervingly close. "Such as?"

"It once belonged to Empress Elizabeth of Russia. We are fairly certain this is true, as my mother was held captive by a Russian who insisted the tiara belonged to him."

"Good heavens."

"Yes, it is quite a story. If you ask Mother, she'll be happy to regale you with the tale. She never tires of sharing how my father came to her rescue."

"I should think so. I would certainly do the same." She moved in front of the fire, preferring its heat to his unsettling warmth. The fireplace didn't distract her nearly as much. "So none of you have ever seen the tiara?"

"No. But we believe it is made of pink diamonds."

Isa froze. "Pink?"

He drew his brows together. "Yes."

"Pink diamonds are rare, are they not?"

"Yes."

She took a step toward him, unable to stop herself in her excitement. "And you believe the painting to be a portrait of your great-great-grandmother wearing the tiara?"

He nodded.

"Is she perhaps wearing a pink gown and holding a dog on her lap?"

"I suppose that is possible, but as you deduced, none of us have ever seen the painting."

"I have."

He rushed to her and grasped her upper arms in an iron grip. "What do you mean?"

Biscuit let out a bark, and Isa wiggled against his slightly painful grasp until he relaxed his fingers. "There is a painting that meets that description in a small gallery not too far from here, in Staffordshire."

His thumbs slid gently back and forth on her arms. Heat rushed through her, reminding her how long it had been since anyone had touched her or attempted to comfort her. George was her only family, and she hadn't seen him in nearly three years. "Are you certain?"

She looked up into his brilliant green eyes. "Of course I cannot be sure, but the lady in the portrait is wearing an unusual tiara made of pink diamonds. That's why I remember it. Because I'd never seen a pink diamond."

He lifted her off the ground and spun her around, eliciting a series of barks from Biscuit. "Do you think you can take us there?" he asked, his mouth so close to her ear that his warm breath floated across it, sending tingles through her.

"Yes, it is not overly difficult to find," she said against his neck, which carried the faint scent of lime.

As if realizing what he had done, he all but dropped her in his haste to disengage. "My apologies, Miss Winthrop. In my excitement, I forgot myself for a moment."

"It's quite all right, my lord." It wasn't, of course, but she was not going to let him know how much his nearness affected her. The weakness in her knees still lingered, and her heart had yet to resume its normal pattern.

"It's just that I've been searching for that tiara for most of my life, and in one moment, you've managed to supplant everything I've done."

Isa swallowed, unsure how to respond. "I assure you it is through no cleverness of my own."

"Well, you've certainly managed to deflate my ego a few levels, which I have no doubt you are pleased about."

She returned his grin.

"The party guests aren't meant to start arriving for a few more days, and even if they were, I don't think I can wait. We must leave as soon as possible and find that painting. Do you think you can lead us to the gallery?"

Isa took a deep breath and waited for her thundering heart to slow. For a second she had allowed herself to get caught up in the excitement of the moment, but she had to remember why she was working so hard. She sent nearly all of the small salary Lady Concord gave her to George to help restore their family estate. The leaky roof had been fixed, but there was no money to refurbish the inside of the house or buy furniture. It was past time for him to marry, but Stowe Hall was uninhabitable in its current state. She could not allow another opportunity to help him pass by.

"Of course, my lord." She clasped her trembling hands together and swallowed her nausea, then forced the words to leave her mouth. "I will take you there for a payment of two-hundred and fifty pounds."

"You'll what?" he roared. "How dare you attempt to extort money from me. You are certainly no lady, but a…a… mercenary."

"That is true. I am not a lady, and I don't intend to spend my life as a lady's companion." She sucked in a deep breath and reminded herself that she was doing this for George. No matter how distasteful her task was, she had to take every opportunity to help him restore honor to his title, to their family. If they could just escape the legacy of their father's actions, she would never be put in this type of situation again. Lord Kenworth had nothing but disdain for her from the moment they met, so it shouldn't matter to her that her actions would permanently cement his dislike of her. "If you wish me to take you to the painting, I require payment. I cannot work for Lady Concord forever. I must consider my future."

Though his face was an alarming shade of red, he spoke calmly enough. "And you think extortion is the best way to do that?" His voice dripped with disdain. "Fine. I'll give you one hundred and fifty pounds."

"Two hundred." She held up her hand as he opened his mouth to argue. "That is my final offer. I know how wealthy your family is. This is pittance to you, and without my help, you'll never locate the gallery."

He sighed. "Very well. Two hundred. Make whatever arrangements you must with Lady Concord so you are free to leave tomorrow. Since I am paying you, I expect you to behave as my servant."

Heat charged up her neck. Did he expect her to polish his boots or lug hot water for his bath? "How am I to do that without alerting the others to our…agreement?"

He shrugged. "I don't particularly care."

"I shall need a chaperone to make the trip with us."

A wicked smile formed on his face, and he looked her up and down as if assessing her merits. "Yes, of course. We wouldn't want anyone to question your integrity." He rolled his eyes. "There is no way Mother will allow me to go on this trip without her, so you needn't worry about your virtue being compromised. At least, certainly not by me."

A thrill ran through her as she allowed herself, for just a moment, to imagine what it would be like to have him study her not out of disgust, but with interest.

He spun on his heel and exited into the corridor. Isa released her pent-up breath. She didn't care a whit what Lord Kenworth thought of her, but she was sorry to involve the duchess in her scheme. Hopefully, the level of excitement the duchess exhibited over finally locating the painting would help outweigh the level of guilt Isa experienced.

She closed her eyes and took a deep breath. Helping George restore his properties and their family honor was her first priority. Nothing else mattered. She had to stay focused on that and not allow herself to be distracted by a presumptuous earl.

Chapter Five

Miss Winthrop glanced at his mother, who was gazing out the window of the carriage and not paying them any heed, then met his malevolent stare with one of her own. He raised a brow but said nothing, daring her to say anything with his mother present. His opinion of her had already been set, and it would not change. Regardless of her situation, a lady did not resort to blackmail. Besides, her position with Lady Concord seemed secure, so there was no logical explanation for her actions. In fact, if anything, she ought to be concerned that her nefarious activities might cause her to lose her position. He sensed there was something more to her story that she hadn't shared, perhaps even something she needed to hide from him.

The most worrisome aspect of the situation was that he did not have two hundred pounds to give her. Despite the wealth of his parents, he received a surprisingly small allowance, and if he didn't choose a bride during the house party, he would be cut off completely. He didn't doubt for a moment that his father would do it. Of course, it remained to be seen whether she was correct that the portrait they were about to see was in fact the one they had sought for so long. Perhaps he wouldn't need to pay her at all.

Mother turned to him. "Darling, why aren't you more excited? I can barely stop myself from bouncing on the seat in anticipation."

For an insane moment, he considered blurting out something about never trusting a blackmailer, but instead he said, "After having followed so many false leads in the past, I find myself skeptical."

"Well, we shall soon find out."

Miss Winthrop closed her book and stretched her arms above her head. "We're almost there."

Despite her lack of integrity, Edward couldn't help but admire her comely figure. At least she had other assets she could parlay into a new career should she lose her position with Lady Concord.

The driver turned the carriage into the entrance to a large estate. The park went on for miles, through rolling hills and expansive gardens as they neared the house. It turned out that the place she spoke of was a gallery curated by the Earl of Marroll, which he kept open to the public. His mother had sent a note upon their arrival in the village the previous evening and had received an enthusiastic response from the earl himself inviting them to tour the gallery this morning.

Mother turned away from the window and focused on Miss Winthrop. "However did you manage to find Lord Marroll's gallery?"

"I accompanied Lady Concord on a visit to her cousin

last summer. She lives quite near here and, during the course of our stay, she brought us to view Lord Marroll's extensive collection."

Mother clasped Miss Winthrop's hand. "What a happy coincidence that you came to us, and that you happened upon the journal and recognized the connection to the painting. It's as if some sort of divine intervention brought you into our lives."

That, or the instincts of a criminal. It seemed too improbable that she could have somehow linked the painting with the journal so easily when they had spent decades chasing false leads and making no progress.

The carriage negotiated the circular drive and stopped in front of an enormous Palladian mansion. A man he presumed to be Lord Marroll emerged from the house and approached the carriage. Edward handed down his mother and reached for Miss Winthrop's hand, but she ignored him and climbed out on her own.

"Lord Marroll, I presume?" Mother held out her hand to him.

"Your Grace." He bowed. "It is a pleasure to have you view my humble gallery."

"We greatly appreciate your hospitality." She quickly introduced Edward and Miss Winthrop.

"Miss Winthrop. How delightful to see you again. You visited last summer with Lady Concord, did you not?"

She curtsied. "Yes, my lord. I am honored you remember me."

"It isn't often that I have visitors with your extensive knowledge of art."

Edward frowned. How had a paid companion become

an expert on art? Perhaps Lady Concord had a large library that she had studied. She was an odd creature. Both a connoisseur of art and a blackmailer.

"Would you like some refreshment, or would you rather go straight to the gallery?"

Mother glanced at Edward and turned back to Lord Marroll. "I think we should like to go to the gallery immediately. As I said in my note, we are very interesting in determining whether you possess a painting of my great-grandmother that once hung in the library at Walsley Manor."

"Very well." He led them around to the side of the main house, where a separate building stood that mirrored the architecture of the residence. Edward moved to open the door and held it until everyone had entered.

There were paintings of every size and type cluttering the walls. Edward could spend days here studying each picture, and if he hadn't been so anxious to find their painting, he would have enjoyed exploring the gallery.

Lord Marroll held out his hand toward the wall closest to them. "My family has been collecting art for several centuries. Because it comes from various sources, it is difficult to determine how to organize the pieces, so over time the gallery has evolved based on the date a particular piece was acquired. In the case of the painting you seek, it is located among the items acquired by my father."

Edward entered the room and spotted the painting immediately. It hung about halfway up the wall, nestled between a landscape and another portrait. A jolt shot through his stomach. There it was. The tiara. The painting was smaller than he had imagined. It would not have filled the space above the fireplace. What if it was the wrong painting?

But no, that had to be the tiara. Surely there couldn't be more than one tiara made with priceless pink diamonds. He glanced at Miss Winthrop, noting the excitement mixed with relief in her eyes.

Mother moved mere inches from the picture and studied every detail. "See her straight-edged nose and the green eyes?" she said to him. "She resembles your grandmother. Or, I guess that would be the other way around."

"Yes, I can see the likeness," Lord Marroll said.

Edward turned to him. "Do you mind if we remove it from the wall so we can look more closely?"

"Of course not." He held out his hand toward the portrait, then walked to the other end of the gallery.

Edward lifted it carefully, making sure the wire didn't catch on the hooks, and was surprised when Miss Winthrop slid past him to help set it safely on the ground. He leaned it against the wall and took in the details. His great-great-grandmother's provocative smile, her similarity to his mother and grandmother, the pink diamonds of the tiara. There seemed to be hundreds of them of various sizes, with the largest at the center. It had to be at least ten carats.

"What are we looking for?" Miss Winthrop asked.

"That is the question, is it not, darling?" His mother placed her hand on his arm. "I don't think there's any question that it is her, but I do not see anything in the painting that will help us determine where the tiara was hidden."

Miss Winthrop tilted her head to the right, as if she needed to examine it from a different angle. "Perhaps the clue isn't in the picture. We should examine the back of the painting."

He exchanged a look with his mother then lifted the painting, turning it around and carefully leaning it so the frame touched the wall to prevent damage. Edward knelt and looked closely. A wood frame outlined the back of the canvas, with two slats connecting from the top to the bottom, presumably to protect the canvas. He couldn't discern whether what he was seeing was the canvas on which the picture had been painted, or a second layer used to protect the first.

"Was there a signature on the front?" he asked.

Mother shook her head.

"Not that I saw," Miss Winthrop added. She leaned close to his mother and they shared a whispered exchange he could not hear before Mother approached Lord Marroll.

"My lord, I cannot thank you enough for allowing us to study the painting. I think it is clear that it is a portrait of my great-grandmother. Would you be so kind as to allow me to purchase the portrait from you so I can return it to its rightful place at Walsley Manor?"

He crossed his arms. "I'm afraid I can't do that."

Mother's smile dipped. "I am prepared to offer you whatever price you demand, even enough to replace it with several other portraits."

Stepping toward her, he said, "No, no, Your Grace, you misunderstand me. I will not sell the painting to you, but I would like to give it to you. It should go back to your home where it belongs."

She shook her head. "That is very generous of you, my lord, but I cannot allow you to do that."

"Of course you can. I shall enjoy searching for another painting to take its place. I'm only sorry that there isn't a way to determine whether any of the other paintings in this chamber came from Walsley."

"You are too kind."

Edward had no doubt that his mother would send him another portrait to take its place. She would insist upon it.

"If you'll excuse me for a moment," Lord Marroll said, "I will fetch a footman to help us wrap the painting and secure it to your carriage properly, so as not to cause any damage."

Edward turned back to where the portrait sat and noted Miss Winthrop studying the back.

She shook her head as he approached. "It's quite odd that there is no signature. Unless the artist signed the back, and there is an extra layer of canvas set over the first."

"We will be able to study the picture more closely once we get back to Walsley. We cannot risk causing damage by attempting to dismantle it here."

"No, of course not," she agreed.

She ran her hand lightly over the canvas. "See here?" She clasped Edward's hand and drew it to the back of the painting. Her soft touch all but caressed his palm, sending a quiver of awareness through him. "There is a slight bump here." She gently guided his hand over the place in question. "It could just be another layer of wood or some such to protect the painting. But it might not be."

Edward turned to meet her eyes. Who was this girl, and why was she so invested in their family mystery? She didn't stand to gain anything by helping them further. He was paying her for leading them to the painting, which she had already done. Was she simply bored and in need of an occupation, or was there something more?

Miss Winthrop cleared her throat and tore her gaze from his. "I so wish we could remove the backing now. I believe the return trip shall seem exceedingly long."

Edward could not argue with that.

Chapter Six

The trip back to Walsley was excruciating. Isa couldn't wait to get her hands on that painting. Resisting the lure of any sort of mystery was impossible for her, and now that she had read the entire diary, she could not rest until the tiara was found. She only hoped that would happen before the upcoming house party ended. It would break her heart not to be involved in finally locating the tiara.

The images of the clues from the journal occupied her mind, and she hadn't realized they were so close to Walsley until the carriage slowed to turn into the drive. She gasped as they approached the house. Three carriages were being unloaded. At least some of the guests had already arrived.

Lord Kenworth straightened and peered through the window. His eyes narrowed. "Mother, you invited Lady Mary?"

"Darling, we couldn't very well hold a house party and not invite Lord Hooksett and his family."

"I don't see why not. It is our party, and we have the right to invite, or not invite, anyone we please."

Her Grace raised her brows at her son, but didn't comment.

"What I don't understand is why, knowing how I feel about her, you would waste an invitation on her. Surely you don't think I'd ever consider marrying her, and Father was very clear about the consequences if I don't choose a bride as a result of this party."

"Darling, you know there are other things that must be considered when preparing a guest list."

Isa bit her lip and kept her gaze trained out the window. They were forcing Lord Kenworth to marry? That at least partly explained why he was so irritable. Lady Concord had not mentioned that there was a purpose to the house party. Isa hadn't known him for long, and she definitely couldn't claim to know him well, but she was certain he would not enjoy trying to weed through a bunch of ladies in a matter of days to determine who was the best option to spend the rest of his life with, though she would certainly enjoy watching him attempt to choose his bride.

His Grace stood in front of the house and opened the door as soon as the carriage came to a halt. Perhaps even before it had.

"Thank goodness you have returned." He unabashedly engulfed his wife in a hug and kissed her soundly on the lips. "Did you locate the portrait?"

She grinned at him and nodded.

"Excellent. Unfortunately, you will have to wait to tell me more because you must assume your hostess duties immediately. If I have to continue to deal with the eager mothers and nervous girls, the party will be cancelled forthwith, and I shall throw everyone out immediately."

The duchess laughed and kissed him on the cheek, then turned back to her son. "Have the portrait moved to my sitting room. There will be too much traffic in the library."

Lord Kenworth nodded, and the duke and duchess headed toward the house. To her surprise, he held out his hand to help her exit the carriage, which she didn't think was a gesture he would normally extend to someone he considered to be his servant. As soon as her foot hit the ground, Biscuit tore around the corner of the house and jumped against her skirts. She knelt to pet him.

"I'm shocked by how much that dog likes you. He's always been sort of vaguely grumpy and more interested in food than human companionship."

She raised a brow. "Have you ever considered the possibility that he may just not like you? He seems very fond of your mother."

Two footmen began removing the luggage from the carriage, and Lord Kenworth shot her a glare then turned to speak to them. "Just a moment," Lord Kenworth said. He untied the portrait and lifted it from the carriage. Without asking, Isa grasped one side and steadied it while he climbed down.

"Here," he said, tilting his head toward the side of the house. "Let's go in through the kitchens. They're closer to my mother's sitting room, and that way we should be able to avoid any wayward party guests."

She nodded. As the son of a duke, he had to have spent much of his life entertaining people and ought to be comfortable with it by now. Though, of course, he did say his father was forcing him to marry, so she supposed his reluctance was understandable.

When they reached the entrance, he leaned against the

wall and balanced the portrait on his thigh so he had a free hand to open the door. She hadn't noticed before, but the muscles in his legs were quite defined, even through the fabric of his breeches. He must ride frequently. Isa loved to ride, but she rarely had a chance anymore, as it was an activity in which Lady Concord no longer engaged.

Lord Kenworth shouldered his way through the door, and Isa followed, noting the looks exchanged between the kitchen staff. A wave of heat washed over them as they drew close to the range. The fact that no one questioned him made her think he entered and exited through the kitchens frequently. A woman she assumed to be the cook stepped toward them.

"My lord, I've just made fresh gingerbread. Shall I bring you some along with tea?"

Biscuit's nose twitched. It smelled so heavenly that Isa feared her nose might twitch as well.

"Thank you, Mrs. West. We are headed for Her Grace's sitting room."

She nodded and cast a curious glance at the picture but said no more.

They left the kitchen and navigated up a staircase and through two corridors before finally reaching their destination.

"Let's set it over here, by the window." They gently placed it on the floor and leaned it against the window seat. Lord Kenworth pulled out a pocketknife and cut the twine, then carefully removed the coarse cloth it had been wrapped with.

He met her eyes. "Mother is probably going to kill me for doing this without her, but let's turn it around and see what we can find."

She grinned. "That's fine with me. I can hardly stand the suspense, and I'm certain I'm not the one who will be in trouble when she discovers what we've done."

He shook his head at her. "That is not a safe assumption. Perhaps I will tell her you pulled the painting apart before I could stop you."

She put her hands on her hips. "You wouldn't!"

He grinned back at her. "I most certainly would. However, no matter what I say, the blame will still be placed on me."

"Do we dare remove the framework?" she asked.

"I think we must. We cannot pull back the canvas unless we are certain there is a second layer."

"Very well." She pulled a small knife from the pocket she had sewn into her gown and knelt in front of the frame. She held the blade above the nail she was about to remove and slanted it toward her, so that if her hand slipped, it would not damage the canvas.

Lord Kenworth placed his hand over hers to stop her. "Didn't anyone teach you never to use a knife like that? If it slips you'll stab yourself."

"Better me than the canvas. I will be fine."

He studied her for several seconds, then held up his hands in surrender. "Very well, but don't say I didn't warn you."

He had touched her more times in the past two days than anyone else had in the past year. Of course it didn't mean anything to him, but it made her long for things she couldn't have. Isa put him from her mind and concentrated on the job at hand. After sliding the thin tip of the point under the edge of the nail, she pulled gently. Lord Kenworth sucked in a breath as the knife slipped, but it was easy enough for her to control it. She tried again, and the nail slid out slightly. After two more tries, the nail slipped out. She continued removing nails until she was able to extract one of the boards.

"Here, let me help." He reached for her knife.

"I appreciate the offer, but I'm afraid your hands are too big."

He crossed his arms. "My hands are too big?"

"Yes. You won't be able to fit your fingers into the corners to reach the nails."

He took a few steps closer, and she felt the heat emanating from him against her back. She shivered.

"Where did you learn to do that?"

"Do what?"

"Use a knife like that."

She glanced back at him. "Ah, well, I've had to learn to be resourceful. There's not always time to wait for help when something needs to be done."

"That's a rather cryptic remark."

Just then, the second slat came off and a bulge appeared in the canvas.

"Oh!"

Lord Kenworth dropped onto his knees next to her. "Since there are definitely two layers of canvas, do you think we should just cut the canvas, or continue removing the slats?"

Isa grimaced. "It's hard to say. This frame,"—she pointed to the framework on the back of the canvas—"may have a structural purpose, or it might have been added solely to secure the second canvas. There's no way to tell unless we remove it."

He cast her a surprised glance. "How do you think we should proceed?"

"Well, there's a chance that the second canvas could

hold a clue as well, so I don't think we should cut it. Let's leave the framework intact on the left side, and remove everything from the right side. Then we'll be able to pull it back and reassess."

He nodded his assent.

Working quickly, she removed the rest of the nails.

She waved her hand toward the canvas. "You do the honors."

Lord Kenworth met her eyes for a moment, then knelt and slowly lifted the canvas. He withdrew a strange piece of yellowed card paper with rectangular holes cut into it.

"What is that?"

"Oh, thank goodness." He placed his hand over his heart. "There's finally something I can contribute. I was beginning to feel inferior in the face of your superior nail removal skills."

She cast her eyes toward the ceiling. "Good grief."

"This," he said as he waved it toward her face, "is a Cardano Grille."

"A what?" She blew a loose lock of hair away from her face and studied the strange thing he held.

"It was designed by Girolamo Cardano in the sixteenth century. You place it over a sheet of paper with writing and the words that appear through the holes reveal a unique message."

"So it's used to hide a secret message within another text."

He nodded.

"Where did you learn that?"

"I am not a simpleton. I studied history at Oxford."

"Just like your father."

He swung around. "How did you know that?"

"Lady Concord and I have been taking tea with your parents. Your mother is fond of talking about both of you. You're very much like him, you know."

"You think so? People usually say I favor my mother."

"I mean in personality and actions, not looks."

He narrowed his eyes. "There you are wrong. I am nothing like him."

She smiled, but refrained from commenting. What he didn't realize was that she didn't mean it as an insult. But she certainly wasn't going to tell him that. The duke was charming and kind, and fiercely protective of his family, including Lord Kenworth, though he didn't seem to understand that. Just then, a maid entered with the tea, and Biscuit awoke from his nap. The scent of the freshly baked gingerbread made her stomach growl.

"Thank you," he said to the maid. With a sardonic look, he asked her, "Are you by chance hungry?"

"Yes." She snatched a piece of the gingerbread and placed it on a plate, then poured two cups of tea and sat down. "What is our next step?"

He finished a mouthful of gingerbread before responding. "Well, once we determine that there is no more information to be gained from the portrait, we need to find a place to hang it."

"Well, yes, but what about the Cardano Grille? Should we assume it is meant to be used on a page from the journal?"

"It's a logical first step."

She nodded, then removed the journal from her pocket and handed it to him. "I'll examine the back of the painting while you experiment with the grille. I would suggest starting with the page that holds the next clue, '*Your beauty is eternal, but may remain unknown.'"*

His head snapped up. "You've memorized the clues?"

"It's not difficult. They aren't particularly long." She took pity on Biscuit and tossed him a piece of gingerbread before kneeling in front of the painting to search for writing or anything else that might be of help to them.

A few moments later, Lord Kenworth spoke. "Well, it's definitely not made to fit this page. Perhaps this clue was given solely to throw us off."

She turned to him. "Are you certain? Did you try turning it in every direction and flipping it over?"

"Yes, Miss Wiseacre. I understand how to use the cipher."

"It's just so disappointing."

"Yes, it is. Now we'll have to try it on every single page in the journal."

Her heartbeat sped up. He had said "we," as in, she would continue to be involved. She turned back to the painting to continue her search, and was surprised when he spoke again. "Do you have any siblings, Miss Winthrop?"

She stiffened. Did he suspect something? "Why do you ask?"

"Just answer me."

"I have an older brother."

He nodded. "I thought so."

"Why?"

"Because you are too good at arguing not to."

A laugh burst from her mouth. "Do you have siblings other than Louisa?"

"Yes, quite a lot of them. I am the oldest, then Caroline and Anne, who are both married, then Louisa, then Henry and Oliver, who are at Eton."

She nodded and tried to imagine what it would be like to have so many siblings. It was for the best that she had not had more brothers or sisters, since it would have been devastating for George to have to assume responsibility for more people. The burden of worrying about her was more than enough.

Isa studied the canvas one last time then sat down on the floor, ready to admit defeat. "I don't think there is anything else to be learned from the painting. I cannot find any writing or other clues."

Lord Kenworth stood and stretched. "I figured as much. It wouldn't make sense if we were able to solve the mystery so easily."

He reached out to her. She placed her hand in his, and he drew her up from the floor. She stood mere inches from him, staring into his emerald eyes, and she couldn't move away. She didn't want to.

After a few moments, he cleared his throat but did not let go of her hand. "If you don't mind my asking, why don't you live with your family?"

This was dangerous territory. She had to choose her words carefully, because she didn't want to lie to him, though of course she could not reveal the entire truth, either.

"I don't. Mind, that is." Disarmed by his regard, she took a deep breath to calm her nerves. "My parents are dead, and my brother cannot afford to keep me. I became Lady Concord's companion to spare him the added burden of having to take care of me."

His eyes widened, but otherwise his face remained neutral. "Lady Concord is very lucky to have you."

Before she could analyze his remarks, the door burst

open, and they shot away from each other. Her Grace glanced at each of them then spoke. "What news do you have? Have you found the tiara yet?"

Isa laughed. "No, but we did find something." She nodded toward Lord Kenworth.

"We have this." He lifted the cipher with a flourish.

"And that is?" she asked.

He explained quickly and caught her up on their progress, or lack thereof, so far. "Now that we've finished examining it, where would you like to hang the painting?"

"Where it belongs. Over the fireplace in the library."

"Won't His Grace mind having the portrait of the two of you replaced?" Isa asked.

The duchess smiled. "I doubt it. He has never liked that painting. Hmmm. Perhaps I shall have it moved to his study."

Isa laughed and turned back to the portrait, quickly tacking the frame back on.

He helped her turn it around. "Do you know where she sat for the painting?" Isa asked. "It doesn't look like the library."

"You're right, Isabella," the duchess said. "In the excitement of finding it, I didn't notice."

Lord Kenworth studied the picture. "There is no such room at Walsley."

Begin where warmth abounds. Very close, yet worlds away, it is no place for the meek. The words ran through Isa's mind, and she wondered if only the first part of the riddle applied to the location of the painting. Perhaps the rest pertained to the cipher.

"Since you will both be occupied with your guests tonight, would you like me to take the cipher and the journal? I should be able to get through it fairly quickly." Though it was unlikely that any of the guests would recognize her, Isa had to be cautious, and delving into the mystery provided the perfect excuse. Besides, she was more interested in finding the tiara than mingling with the ladies who were hoping to marry Lord Kenworth.

"Isabella, you are one of our guests. You may not hide in your room. The tiara has been missing for decades. We can wait one more night."

"You are very kind, Your Grace, but—"

"I shall take it as a personal insult if you don't at least join us for dinner."

Isa bit back a smile. "Yes, Your Grace." Because of their family situation, George had never invited his friends to join him during school holidays, and Isa had never made her come out and been introduced to society, so the chances of her being recognized here, among a group of wealthy members of the *ton*, were very slim. Still, she had to be careful, because she could not afford to lose her position with Lady Concord.

"Besides," the duchess continued, "Edward has been searching for the tiara since he was old enough to understand what it was, and we don't want to deprive him of the satisfaction of finding it." She turned and walked to the doorway. "Both of you need to go get some rest. I will have the paintings moved."

Once his mother had walked farther down the corridor, he turned to Isa. "There's no point in protesting. Once she makes up her mind about something, there is no changing it." He picked up the journal and slid the cipher into it, then held out his hand toward her. "After you."

So that was it. She would have to attend dinner after all, and pray that no one would recognize her.

Chapter Seven

E dward would rather be subjected to a year of nonstop lectures from his father than go downstairs and mingle with the ladies who had been invited for his inspection. He shuddered at the thought of their mothers, who were worse than the simpering girls. There was no point in delaying further. None of them were going anywhere. After one last attempt to tame his hair, he moved out into the corridor and nearly collided with Miss Winthrop.

"I beg your pardon, my lord."

"The fault is mine." He held out his hand to indicate she should precede him. Lady Concord and her companion had been placed into the rooms in the family wing that had once belonged to Caroline and Anne, in order to make more room for the other guests who had been invited to the house party.

"Shouldn't you already be at the party?"

"Have you been conspiring with my parents?"

She laughed. "Of course not, but I had to help Lady Concord before I could ready myself, and I thought I was late."

He found her quite alluring in a simple light blue gown that set off her eyes and suspected that she would attract the attention of the other gentlemen, at least until they found out she had no dowry or connections. A glimpse of her profile put him in mind of someone, but he couldn't remember whom. The fleeting image escaped him.

"Not to worry. If we were late, Mother would have sent someone to fetch us."

Edward continued to be surprised that Miss Winthrop had not yet demanded he pay her for leading them to the painting. Perhaps she wasn't as mercenary as he had originally thought. From what he understood of her background, she likely needed the money. However, he did not countenance blackmail and would not offer her the agreed upon sum unless she asked. If necessary, he was certain he could convince his mother to loan him the required amount. Nonetheless, the fact that she actually needed the money lessened his dislike of her. He was cognizant of the fact that he had grown up in a world of wealth and privilege, so he had no experience with how unsettling it would be to have an unsure future. He might actually have liked her had they met under different circumstances.

Walsley was old and had been built on the side of a hill. It was a bit of a hodgepodge, with parts that resembled a castle and others more like a manor house. The worn, uneven stone steps could be difficult to maneuver. He drew Miss Winthrop's arm through his as they followed the sounds from the party, moving up and back down several staircases before they made their way into the banqueting hall. Long tables, already set for dinner, flanked each wall. Not one to waste opportunities, Mother had hired musicians so they could dance after dinner, and they were already settled in the minstrel's gallery.

Miss Winthrop removed her arm from his. "Thank you for your assistance, my lord."

He inclined his head. For a moment her withdrawal left him feeling oddly alone in a room full of people.

She looked up at the detailed plasterwork on the vaulted ceiling. "This is such an unusual chamber. Every house should have one like this." Though he hadn't known her for long, she never failed to say something that surprised him. Most people found the house odd at best.

Gorham waved to him from the other side of the room and he shot her a smile before leaving her to her own devices.

"How are you holding up?" his friend asked.

"As well as can be expected, considering that I'm being treated like a stallion forced to choose a mate."

"We should all be so unfortunate." He slapped him on the back. "Take a look around you. Only you could be unhappy about being surrounded by beautiful ladies with large dowries."

Gorham knew well enough about the number of times one of these so-called ladies had attempted to force him into a compromising position, hoping it would lead to a marriage proposal. In fact, it reminded him that he needed to keep his bedchamber locked for the duration of the house party. "I give you my permission to pursue anyone who catches your fancy. Consider it my way of saying thank you for attending and helping to direct some of the attention away from me."

"Is it just me, or does Lady Mary remind you of that maid from Oxford? The one with the red hair."

"No wonder I never warmed to Lady Mary. My father nearly made me come home after I was caught in the library with the maid." Edward was not proud of his behavior, but he certainly hadn't been the only one who had partaken of her readily offered charms.

The weight of his father's stare reminded him of the expectations of his parents, and he forced himself to move around the room and greet everyone.

"Lady Lydia, Lady Mary, how lovely to see you here. I trust you find your accommodations to your liking?"

"Yes, my lord."

The girls were twins, just sixteen years old. Mary always spoke for both of them. He wasn't sure if Lydia was too shy to speak or just didn't like him. He had thought Mary was a nice girl, and she was passably attractive, but she had attempted to trap him in the cloak-room at a ball in London, and he had avoided her ever since.

"I hope you enjoy dinner. Her Grace has some surprises in store for everyone tonight." He winked at them and moved on. Good lord. He felt like a street seller hawking his wares.

He spotted Miss Winthrop standing with Lady Helen and made his way over to them. "Lady Helen, Miss Winthrop. Are you enjoying yourselves?"

"Very much, my lord," said Lady Helen. A deep blush immediately colored her face, as it did every time she spoke with him or any other gentleman. He admired her courage in making the effort to socialize, considering how uncomfortable she seemed to be. He reminded himself to be sure to dance with her after dinner.

Miss Winthrop's eyes widened slightly when she noted Lady Helen's discomfort, then she jumped into the conversation. "We are having a lovely discussion about *The Amber Witch*. Have you read it, my lord?"

"I'm afraid not. Isn't that the German book that was supposed to have been based on a manuscript written by a minister from the sixteen hundreds?"

Her brows shot up. "Why yes, my lord. How clever of you to know. You should consider reading it. I believe it will soon gain popularity." She turned to her companion. "Don't you think so, Lady Helen?"

"Yes, of course. It is an excellent story, regardless of its provenance."

How remarkable. She did not blush when she kept her focus on Miss Winthrop. It would be interesting to know if the reaction was only for him, or if it was just men in general.

Thankfully, the dinner bell rang and they all moved to take their places at the two long tables that flanked the walls of the room. Half of the young ladies and their mothers had been assigned to his table, and half to the table with his parents. He imagined the seating would be rotated each evening. He noted that Miss Winthrop and Lady Helen were seated together at his parents' table and surmised that his mother had deliberately arranged it that way since, of course, Miss Winthrop was not a candidate for marriage.

B y the time the fourth course had arrived, Edward had begun to wonder whether his parents had deliberately rounded up the most hideous group of girls they could find to punish him for every misdeed he had ever committed and more. Lady Lydia was the opposite of her twin sister, and so appallingly boring he considered stabbing himself with a knife just so he had an excuse to leave the table.

"What do you think about the talk of changing crop rotation cycles, my lord?"

Clearly, someone had told her that men would be attracted to women who could help manage their estates. He had to admire her for attempting to resuscitate the conversation. "I admit I haven't thought much about the subject, though I'm certain my father has many opinions." Lady Helen proceeded to debate both sides of the issue, primarily with herself, as most of the rest of the occupants of his table appeared to be sleeping with their eyes open.

Several millennia later, the dessert course was served, and he was finally free. For about a minute and a half. Then the dancing began.

As the daughter of a duke, Lady Phoebe was the highest ranking unmarried woman, so he approached her first. "Lady Phoebe." He bowed over her hand. "Would you care to join me for the first dance?"

"Of course, my lord."

They took their place at the end of the room and waited for the musicians. She was extraordinarily beautiful. Her face was perfectly proportioned, and her golden brown eyes shimmered below her smooth blond hair. Yet she failed to stir any sort of response from him. She was like a china doll. Beautiful on the outside but empty on the inside, where it mattered. Miss Winthrop, on the other hand, had turned out to have much more substance to her than he had anticipated.

"My lord, Her Grace has informed me that you have made progress in locating a lost family heirloom. I imagine that must be very exciting for you."

What an odd subject for Mother to speak about over dinner. Perhaps the conversation at her table had been as lacking as that at his. However, since he did not wish to discuss the tiara with her, he changed the topic. "Yes, it is. And I have heard that you have purchased a new mare that is the talk of London."

"Indeed, my lord. She is a bonny ride, with a trot that is simply divine to sit." She winked at him, and his skin grew hot. Could she be hinting at what he assumed she was hinting at? He thought his chums had been engaging in wishful thinking when they said that women could experience intense pleasure while riding. It certainly wasn't the case for men; if anything, they were likely to injure themselves.

She really was quite perfect, aside from the fact that, as the daughter of a solvent duke, she knew she could get away with just about anything, and she had. Rumor had it among his friends from Oxford that she would not be entering the marriage bed with her virginity intact. After growing up with the example of a mother and father who had made a love match, he wasn't about to marry a woman who would never remain faithful to him.

He watched as his father led Mother around the dance floor. She laughed at something he whispered in her ear, and he pulled her closer. That was the sort of relationship he wanted, and if he wasn't able to find the right woman, he would not marry. It couldn't be forced, and he refused to choose one as if he were selecting a horse from an auction, which is what this party really was.

Lady Phoebe continued to extoll the virtues of her horse, but his attention was caught by the sound of Miss Winthrop's laughter joined by a laugh he knew all too well. Thornbrook. He should have known better than to invite him. He was a loyal friend and great fun in most situations, but he had a knack for seeking out the ladies who were the most vulnerable. Though he usually went for those who were both wealthy and beautiful, but lacked proper supervision, that did not mean he would pass up the opportunity to take advantage of a lady who was on her own. In any case, Edward would warn her off from him after the dancing ended, and then make sure that Thornbrook had been properly introduced to Lady Phoebe. They ought to get along swimmingly.

Thankfully, the music finally ended and he murmured something polite before turning to look for Miss Winthrop. Instead, he caught the eye of his mother, who tilted her head toward Lady Sarah. He sighed and walked over to her.

"Lady Sarah, I was afraid I might not have the opportunity to dance with you tonight. Will do you do me the honor of saving the next dance for me?"

"Of course, my lord."

Of all his mother's carefully chosen candidates, she was the most perfect. She was pretty, but not beautiful enough to use it as a weapon, very agreeable, and from a family with no dark secrets. If only he could drum up some sort of attraction to her.

"Are you enjoying yourself?"

"Very much so, my lord. I'm fascinated by Walsley. There are so many architectural styles, yet somehow they blend together into a most enchanting home."

He shot her a genuine smile. "I could not agree with you more."

He frowned when Miss Winthrop once again lined up with Thornbrook.

"Is something amiss, my lord?"

"No." He shot her a smile. "Would you be interested in touring the grounds with me tomorrow? They are even more interesting than the house."

"That I find difficult to believe, but yes, I would love to."

There. Now his parents could not accuse him of not making an effort to choose a bride from among the ladies they invited. It would not be his fault if she left engaged to someone else. She was perfect for Gorham, and he would make sure to invite him on their tour.

It was a country dance that was played next, and he had to pay careful attention just to keep up. He had mostly avoided balls when they were in London, so he was out of practice. At one point, he turned the wrong way and nearly caused an accident. Thankfully, Lady Sarah was tolerant of his mistakes. In fact, he caught her laughing at him more than once, which was refreshing, as most ladies gave him absolute deference. He could respect a lady who didn't attempt to fawn over him and say what she thought he wanted to hear.

When the dance finally, blessedly, ended, he took her hand and led her to the side of the room. "My lady, I must apologize for my atrocious dancing tonight. I have no excuse other than lack of practice, but I hope you will still join me for that tour of the gardens tomorrow."

"Of course, my lord. Think nothing of it."

Gorham happened to be walking by at that moment and appeared to be en route to Miss Winthrop. With no subtlety whatsoever, Edward snagged his sleeve. "Lady Sarah, have you had the pleasure of meeting Lord Gorham? We were at Oxford together."

"Yes, of course. We met earlier. How do you do, my lord?"

"I am well, thank you. Her Grace just announced that this will be the last dance of the evening, a waltz. Would you care to join me?"

"It would be my pleasure."

Edward smiled, satisfied with his matchmaking efforts, then rushed over to Miss Winthrop. "Can I interest you in joining me for the last dance of the evening?"

She smiled one of her genuine smiles. Though they had only known each other for a few days, he already knew the difference between her authentic smile and her placating smile. It occurred to him that should be a warning of some sort, but he chose to ignore it.

"I suppose it would be churlish to refuse the guest of honor."

"It most certainly would." As he exhaled, he relaxed for the first time that night. Now he could drop the act and simply be himself. From the moment the first note sounded, they were in perfect harmony with each other. Miss Winthrop was an accomplished dancer and a pleasure to partner. Of course, he didn't have to concentrate to remember the steps of the waltz.

"You seemed to enjoy dancing with Lord Thornbrook." He raised a brow.

"Is that a question, my lord?"

"More of an observation, I guess."

She turned to meet his eyes. "He is a proficient dancer and an excellent conversationalist."

"Is he now?"

"I would think you of all people would know that. He claims to be one of your closest acquaintances." This time she raised her brows.

"Yes, he is an excellent friend to me, but not the sort of man I would want to date one of my sisters."

Her face flooded with color. "I am *not* one of your sisters, my lord."

"Believe me, I am quite aware of that, but I still feel the need to warn you against him as I would any lady for whom I have regard."

"I cannot believe that you…wait. You have regard for me?"

Ahem. Perhaps he should have chosen his words more carefully. "Of course I have regard for the lady who helped us find the missing puzzle piece in our quest to locate the tiara."

"Oh." Her face fell for a moment, then she plastered on a fake smile. "You needn't worry about me. The circumstances of my life have caused me to become an excellent judge of character. I recognize your friend for what he is."

"My apologies. I did not mean to offend you." He pulled her a little closer and focused on his steps, unsure how to fix whatever he had done to upset her. He had no idea why his attempt to protect her was offensive. It seemed prudent to remain quiet.

A few moments later, she said, "It is I who should apologize, my lord. I appreciate you taking an interest in my welfare."

He nodded. Her words seemed sincere, but her dejected tone threw him off. She was as complicated as any of his sisters, but he had learned his lesson about comparing her to one of them. Silence was preferable to offending her again.

Finally, the dance came to an end. He took her hand to lead her back to Lady Concord, but he wasn't able to locate her. "Where is Lady Concord?"

"Oh, she headed back to her bedchamber at least an hour ago. You probably didn't notice since you were busy dancing."

Was that a note of censure in her voice? Surely not. He shook his head to clear it. "Either wait for me, or walk back to your room with my parents or Louisa."

Her eyes narrowed. "You don't need to worry about me. I've been taking care of myself for a long time."

He glanced back over his shoulder and gave her a warning look. He had to say good night to his guests, but it wouldn't take long.

"Very well, *my lord*."

Or had she said, my liege? He bit back a grin. Either way, he had coaxed a smile out of her and a promise not to walk through the house alone. It was probably an unnecessary precaution, but all of the other unmarried ladies had a chaperone with them, so she was the most vulnerable with only an elderly lady for protection, and sometimes, like now, not even that. It wasn't as if he thought any of their guests might attack her, but he had no idea how vulnerable she was to persuasion, and it was his job as the host to ensure her safety.

Edward knocked on the door to his mother's sitting room, then opened it without waiting for a response.

She glanced up at him and smiled. "Come in, darling. Did you enjoy the evening?"

"Not particularly, though there were a few memorable moments."

He sat in the chair across from her and rubbed his forehead. "Why are we continuing this farce? What do you hope the outcome of this party to be, because I don't believe you expect me to marry any of these ladies."

"What is wrong with Lady Phoebe or Lady Sarah?"

"There is nothing at all wrong with Lady Sarah, except that I don't have the slightest attraction to her. As for Lady Phoebe, let's just say that some of my chums are a bit more familiar with her than they ought to be."

Her mouth opened, but no sound emerged.

For once, he had managed to shock his mother, but he was too worn out to savor his victory.

"Surely not."

"I'm afraid so. As the daughter of a duke, she knows she can get away with almost anything and will still receive offers of marriage."

"Is this the sort of behavior you would condone in your sisters?"

He straightened in his seat. "I would hope you know me better than that."

She placed her elbow on the arm of the chair and rested her head in her hand. "Yes, of course I do, darling. I'm sorry. It's been such a long day."

"And I'm sorry to extend it further, but I wanted to speak with you."

She watched him, waiting for him to continue.

"What is this house party really about? You and Father

married for love, and I know you want the same for me. Why are you forcing the matter? Why now?"

"Because we are concerned for your welfare." She sighed. "I chose the guest list carefully. Of course we don't want to force you to marry a woman you don't love, but we do want to see you settled in your own household. Soon."

"I will marry if and when I find the right woman, and if I never do, then Henry or Oliver can assume the title upon my death."

"You needn't be so dramatic. But I do ask that you seriously consider the ladies who are here. I chose each of them for a reason, and aside from Lady Phoebe, any of them would be a wonderful match for you."

He smiled at her exclusion of Lady Phoebe.

"Have you made any progress with the Cardano Grille?"

"Not yet, but I haven't had much time to test it."

She yawned and rose from her chair. "Don't stay up all night working with the grille. It can wait. You will need your wits about you tomorrow to manage our guests."

A truer statement had never been spoken. His head ached at the thought of another two weeks with all these people underfoot, slowing his progress in finally locating the tiara.

Rather than going to his bedchamber, where he would undoubtedly fall asleep quickly, he went to the library so he could work on deciphering the journal. Thankfully, no one else was there, so he settled himself in front of the fireplace with the journal and a glass of port.

He hadn't made much progress when the door creaked open.

"My lord, how delightful to find you here. I couldn't

sleep, so I thought I'd look for something to read." Lady Phoebe closed the door firmly behind her then sauntered into the library. In her dressing gown.

He leaped to his feet. Anger coursed through him with each beat of his heart. How dare she try to trap him. "Lady Phoebe, in case you have forgotten, you are not dressed appropriately to be wandering around the house. I must insist that you return to your chamber at once."

She licked her lips and pouted. "Fine, I will leave. But only if you walk me back to my bedchamber." She approached him, and he stood frozen, like a mouse being stalked by a cat.

Finally, he found his voice. "I will do no such thing. Leave. Now." When she didn't comply, he pushed past her and threw the door open. Miss Winthrop jumped back to avoid being hit by the door. He took a step into the corridor and held up his hand to indicate she should stay where she was, partially hidden behind the door.

"Lady Phoebe, the corridor is clear, you may now leave."

"Must I?" She rubbed her hand over his chest.

"Yes." He removed her hand and pulled her into the corridor, then pushed firmly against her back to get her headed in the right direction. After a few steps, she glanced back over her shoulder and said, "Don't leave me waiting too long, my lord."

He took a deep breath and turned to Miss Winthrop, whose expression had turned from bewilderment to disgust.

"My apologies, my lord. If I had known you scheduled your assignations in the library, I most certainly would have stayed away." She turned and attempted to rush back down the corridor.

Edward caught her arm and turned her to him. "You must allow me to explain."

"There is no need. I saw enough to discern the situation."

"You are mistaken. Please come into the library."

"No, thank you."

At his wits' end, he lifted her into his arms and strode into the library, slamming the door behind him and unceremoniously dropping her onto the settee.

"How dare you touch me after you—"

"After I what? I did not have an assignation, or anything else, with Lady Phoebe."

She crossed her arms and continued to glare at him. "You could have fooled me."

"I appreciate your faith in my character. Nevertheless, I was in here working on the journal when she came in. I forced her to leave immediately."

"Then why did you make me hide behind the door?" "Because if she had known you were there, she would have accomplished her goal of forcing me to make an offer for her." He yanked off his cravat and dropped into a chair.

"Oh."

She chewed on her bottom lip, drawing his attention to her mouth. His stomach tightened. How had he not noticed before how full her lips were?

"Why would she do that?"

"You mean besides to marry someone who will one day be a duke? Or do you find me so repellant that you can't imagine anyone ever wanting to marry me?"

"Don't be ridiculous. You're not repellant." She stood up and moved in front of the fireplace and turned to face him. "You're certainly overbearing and self-important, but in any case, I don't understand why the daughter of a duke would need to resort to trickery. It's not as if there aren't plenty of men who would be willing to marry her."

Momentarily distracted by the way the fireplace outlined her curves through the thin fabric of her gown, he failed to respond.

She frowned. "My lord, my apologies for assuming the worst of you. It was just such a strange situation to witness."

"Thank you. And my apologies for tossing you onto the settee, but it was important to me that you know the truth about what had happened. Or rather, what did not happen."

She nodded and resumed chewing her lip. For an absurd moment, he contemplated soothing it with kisses. Good grief. He needed to go to bed and end the evening before he got himself into any more trouble.

"Did you have a reason for coming down here? I thought you had retired for the night after I walked you to your bedchamber."

"Not really. I just wasn't ready to retire yet. Have you had any luck with the journal?"

He shook his head. "I haven't had time to work on it." Lifting it from the table where he had left it, he flopped onto the settee and pulled out the grille. "I'll try to get through a few pages while you choose a book, and we can walk back together. Heaven knows who might be skulking about the house at this time of night."

After a quick glance at the page, he highly doubted there was a clue to be revealed in this entry. Nevertheless, he applied the grille just as he had on every other page. He glanced up when Miss Winthrop sat next to him. "Have you found a book?"

"Not yet." She pointed to the books on the table. "I haven't been able to narrow it down."

Edward went back to reading the journal.

"What new surprises will my lover have for me tonight?"

He shifted and glanced at Miss Winthrop, but she appeared to be absorbed in her book.

"I long for the sweet torture of his touch, for the pleasure he brings me."

Sitting next to her was becoming a form of torture, as he imagined giving her pleasure, wishing he could discover her most sensitive places. He shook his head and attempted to focus on finding the clue, but the grille revealed the words "throb," "craving," and "attention."

It was just his luck that Miss Winthrop chose that moment to check on him.

She glanced at the page. "Have you found anything... Oh." Obviously she remembered the passage, since she blushed immediately. "I shouldn't think that section would hold a clue."

He grinned. "I agree, but we must be thorough, which means checking each and every page of the journal, even the, er, saucy entries."

"Yes, of course we must be meticulous." Still refusing to meet his eyes, she cast her glance toward the floor.

"I'm sorry, Miss Winthrop. I did not intend to make you uncomfortable." He closed the journal.

She placed her hand on his and sent a jolt through him, despite the fabric of her glove between them. "No, my lord. It is not your fault. If I hadn't already read the journal, I would never have recognized the passage. It was quite... surprising the first time I read it."

"Yes, I imagine so." Edward shifted again and glanced at her, wondering if her skin was as smooth as it looked. He wanted to trace the delicate line of her jaw and press his lips against the pulse in her neck, and…and it was time to leave. He leaped off the settee.

"Have you chosen a book?"

She met his eyes. "I'll just take them all."

He picked up her stack of books and opened the door for her. They made their way to the family wing of the house in silence. When they reached the door to her bedchamber, he stopped. "Thank you for not automatically condemning me after the incident with Lady Phoebe, Miss Winthrop." He bowed to her.

"You're welcome, my lord." She curtsied and shot him a grin. He handed her the books, and she disappeared into her chamber.

He thanked the stars she hadn't been privy to his thoughts in the library. Though there was no logical explanation for it, he was pleased not to have lost her regard. Perhaps it meant more to him because she was one of the few people who had nothing to gain by offering him false compliments.

Chapter Eight

Despite having stayed up much later than was usual for her, Isa woke up at the same time as any other day. The incident with Lord Kenworth and Lady Phoebe last night flooded her mind, and for a moment, she thought it must have been a dream. Though she knew ladies could be compromised all too easily, she had never imagined that one would set out to deliberately compromise herself in order to make an advantageous match. No doubt there were few who would resort to such drastic measures, but it gave her a new appreciation for the pressures Lord Kenworth faced. Of course, his situation was so much more advantageous than hers that she could hardly feel sorry for him, but at least now she understood him better.

Thankfully George would never have to worry about that sort of thing. As the dinner progressed last night, she had become more certain that no one attending the house party would recognize her. She had spent very little time in

London as a child and had been only fifteen when her father fled the country to avoid his investors. It had been four years since she accepted the position with Lady Concord, so if anything, she was more likely to be recognized as her companion than the daughter of Lord Stowe.

She broke her fast with Lady Concord in her bedchamber, then headed down to the library with Biscuit at her heels. Aside from the servants, the other occupants of the house seemed to all still be asleep.

After making herself comfortable on the settee, she studied the new portrait over the mantle. She couldn't help but think that they were missing some sort of important hint within the picture. What if the grille was simply a ploy to keep them from moving forward? She didn't see any way that both the grille and the second clue from the journal could be relevant to the solution.

Footsteps sounded in the corridor, and she knew who it was without looking. He entered and sat beside her. Biscuit stretched and sidled over to greet him.

"I hadn't expected to see anyone else up so early." He pulled the journal from his pocket and set it on the table in front of her.

"No luck yet?" she asked.

He shook his head. "I need more time to check all of the pages."

"Though I know you are reluctant to accept it, my offer to help still stands." She turned away from his questioning gaze and pointed toward the fireplace. "What do you see when you look at the portrait?"

"I assume you mean other than my great-great-grandmother and the tiara."

She didn't respond. They both studied the picture. There was still something about the painting that bothered her. Why would she have had her portrait made in a place other than her own home? It required many hours to sit for a painting. Surely she would not have wanted to spend that much time somewhere else. Unless the background of the picture was a clue.

Lord Kenworth shrugged. "What do you think is wrong with it?"

"I don't know yet, but there's something that's not right."

He stood and paced to the window, then paused there and studied the landscape while drumming his fingers against the sill. His behavior this morning was odd. He seemed restless, though perhaps he was just frustrated with their lack of progress with the search.

"I am giving a tour of the gardens this afternoon. Will you come?"

Isa frowned. "It's not the sort of activity Lady Concord would attend. She is no longer able to cover large distances."

He turned back toward her, and she met his eyes. Something had changed between them, but she wasn't sure what. Her heart stuttered, and she turned away from his intense gaze.

"You needn't worry about that. My mother does not plan to attend the garden tour and has invited Lady Concord to play cards with her this afternoon."

"I ought to stay with my employer." She had meant to sound firm, but instead her statement came out more like a question, like she was inviting him to persuade her to join the tour. Though she was grateful that the duchess attempted to include her in the activities of the house party, her effort was wasted. Isa was no longer a part of the world of the aristocracy, and she likely never would be again. If she was lucky, she might someday marry a country squire and live a quiet life away from all of this, but that was the most she could hope for, and there was no point in pretending otherwise.

"I would like for you to be there."

She turned and studied him. There was something in his eyes, something vulnerable that had not been there before. He ruined the effect when he clasped his hands under his chin and batted his eyelashes like the worst sort of coquette. Try as she might, she could not contain her laughter. "Why are you so set on my attending?"

"I need an ally. Without my parents chaperoning, I am vulnerable to the advances of the ladies."

She pursed her lips and glared at him.

"Because I'm afraid you will commandeer the journal, solve the riddle, and locate the tiara without me."

She bit back a smile. "That excuse is at least believable."

"Because there ought to be one other sensible person present. I need someone to look after my interests and protect me from the meddling mamas and ambitious ladies."

"Surely there cannot be other ladies in attendance willing to compromise themselves in order to make a good match. But just in case, perhaps you ought to follow your parents' wishes and apply yourself to choosing your wife before you find yourself stuck with one not of your choosing."

He drew his brows together and was quiet for several moments. "I have already determined that none of these ladies meet my expectations. Hence the need for my own chaperone. Please? Louisa will be there, and you can spend most of your time with her."

"Since you are clearly determined to have me attend for some unknown reason, I will. But don't view this as an indication that I will continue to humor your whims. If I thought I could get my hands on the journal, I wouldn't hesitate to refuse you."

"As I am well aware. Thank you."

He definitely wanted her to participate in the garden tour, and she intended to figure out why.

Isa smoothed her simple cotton gown. It certainly couldn't be compared to the expensive attire of the other ladies present, but she liked it, and that was all that mattered. It wasn't as if she was competing with them for Lord Kenworth's hand. Staying at the back of the group allowed her the chance to explore. The others remained as close as possible to Lord Kenworth while he explained the layout of the gardens.

"Because of the position of the house, it is possible to exit on different levels depending on which side of the house you leave from. We shall explore the lower gardens first, but had we exited from the north side, we would now be in the rose gardens at the top of the hill."

While the rest of the party admired the formal gardens, Isa and Biscuit focused on the wildflowers that had been allowed to grow at the edge of the path. She lost track of time as they wandered farther away from the rest of the group. Footsteps sounded on the gravel path, and she noted Lord Kenworth walking toward her. She bit back a smile.

"I love that the gardener allows the wildflowers to flourish alongside the formal gardens."

"It is my mother's doing. Wildflowers are her favorite, despite the fact that the buttercups make my father sneeze."

"If that isn't a sign of his love, I don't know what is." She ran her hand along a honeysuckle vine and leaned in to catch the heady fragrance of the flower. "This is my favorite."

He moved to stand directly behind her. "So that is the perfume you wear. The scent is so subtle on you I couldn't place it." Her stomach quivered. He drew in a deep breath, and she wasn't sure if he was sniffing her or the flowers.

"I'm afraid I cannot afford to purchase perfume, so the scent comes from the soap we make at Concord House."

"It is a lovely scent on you."

She spun around and he was so close, he reached out to steady her. A frisson shot through her. She swallowed and looked up into the storm of his emerald eyes. Why was he attempting to charm her? What could he want from her?

"Miss Winthrop," he said, but was interrupted by the arrival of Louisa.

"Edward, you are needed to solve a dispute about the growth cycle or some such nonsense." Louisa gestured toward the topiary garden.

"Couldn't you have handled it?"

"Perhaps, but I didn't want to. Besides, the squabbling of the ladies is intended to attract your attention, not mine."

"Is that what women think? That men enjoy watching them fight among themselves?"

"I'm sure I don't know." She turned to Isa, who stood quietly, watching their exchange. "Would you like to walk down to the footbridge? I can show you the place where

Edward nearly drowned while attempting to catch a fish."

"Good lord," Lord Kenworth mumbled while he walked slowly toward the ladies involved in the disagreement. Isa did not envy him his task.

She slid her arm through Louisa's. "I would greatly enjoy exploring the footbridge."

They negotiated a set of narrow stairs built into the hill, then strode onto the bridge. Biscuit stopped at the end of the path and barked at them.

Louisa smiled. "I think he objects to the way the moving water is visible though the spaces between the slats of wood."

"Poor darling. You'll just have to wait there for me." She glanced around. "What a charming location. I imagine you spent much time here as children."

Louisa nodded. "Especially Edward and the other boys. I never quite had the stomach for catching fish. It seemed so cruel to remove them from such an idyllic place and eat them. Instead, I would sneak crumbs from the kitchen to feed them, and they became so tame everyone agreed it wasn't fair to catch them. Now the boys fish in the ponds farther afield and, when they're feeling adventurous, in the River Wye."

Isa grinned. "That sounds like something I would have done to my brother."

"Miss Winthrop—"

"Please, call me Isabella."

"I would be delighted. Isabella, aside from acting as Lady Concord's companion, you seem no different from the other ladies attending the party."

Isa supposed that was true, but she tensed as she waited for Louisa to continue her question. "I thank you for the compliment, and I'm pleased that I have not embarrassed Lady Concord with my conduct."

Louisa clasped her arm. "That is not at all what I meant. It's just that…if I'm not being too impertinent, why are you working as a companion?"

"It is very simple. My father made some unwise investment decisions and left my brother in debt. Both of my parents are now gone, and I don't wish to be a burden to my brother, so I chose to accept a position with Lady Concord. Unfortunately, it is not an usual situation for untitled gentlemen to find themselves in." Though she felt it necessary to mislead Louisa to protect herself and her brother, she had not told a lie. What she had said about untitled gentlemen was true; it just happened that her brother was not one of them.

"You are very brave to go out on your own and also very kind to help your brother."

"Yes, well, one does what she can to help her family." Except she didn't feel much like she was helping anyone. Instead, she thought only of all of the half-truths she had told Louisa and the duchess…and Lord Kenworth. She had placed herself in an impossible situation, and there didn't seem to be a way out of it without revealing her identity. Which would also reveal her duplicity. She paced to the middle of the bridge and gazed into the water. "Now, if you don't mind, I would like to hear the story of your brother's near drowning."

"It's not nearly as exciting as it sounds, but we all enjoy ribbing him about it." She turned to face the other side of the bridge. "He hooked one of the larger fish, but the line got caught under a rock and broke, and he didn't want to leave the fish with the hook in its mouth, so he jumped in and swam after it."

Isa tried to picture Lord Kenworth doing that, and to her surprise, it wasn't a stretch for her to imagine him trying to save a fish.

"The trouble came when his boot caught between two rocks. The current in the creek can be very strong, especially after it rains. As I'm sure you know, it is nearly impossible to remove riding boots when they are wet. Luckily, Papa was nearby and was able to haul him out."

Isa's heart pounded as if the event was unfolding before her. "How old was he when this happened?"

"He was home on break from Eton, so maybe twelve or thirteen? In truth, I'm not old enough to remember when it happened, but we all enjoy teasing him about risking his life to save a fish."

Instead of coming across as an irresponsible mistake, it made Isa respect him more.

Footsteps crunched on the gravel path behind them. The rest of the guests followed along behind Lord Kenworth like ducklings behind their parents.

He sped up, increasing the distance between himself and his flock. "I have no doubt you've already given Miss Winthrop an exaggerated account of my fish story. Will I be allowed to provide a rebuttal?"

Isa spoke before Louisa could respond. "That won't be necessary, my lord. Your sister's story did much to raise my esteem of you. I'm afraid your version of the story might erase that small gain."

He glanced around and lowered his voice. "In that case, please, I beg you, join us for the picnic Mother has arranged for us. I must hear sensible conversation from someone, or I fear for my sanity."

Isa and Louisa exchanged glances and followed him across the bridge before the rest of the party caught up with them. Servants were setting out the picnic in the shade of the trees at the edge of the family cemetery. Biscuit barked and whined pitifully from the other side of the creek. Isa took pity and went back to fetch him and carry him across the bridge.

"I think you might have to take him with you when you leave, or he will be heartbroken," Lord Kenworth commented.

Isa smiled. "Given my circumstances, that isn't possible, but I imagine he will settle back into his former routine as soon as I leave."

"Don't count on it," he said softly. For a moment, his features softened, as if he had dropped his defenses. "You have changed his outlook on life, and it is likely too late to change it back."

Louisa stared at her brother. "Are we still talking about Biscuit?"

"Yes, of course. Who else would we be discussing?"

Lord Kenworth watched while the others broke into smaller groups and settled themselves to enjoy the picnic. Louisa found a spot and waved to Isa, and she and Biscuit joined her, along with Lady Sarah and Lady Helen. He kept watch until all of his guests had found a place to dine, then he sat down between Isa and Lady Sarah.

"What a pleasure to have your company, my lord," Lady Sarah said.

Though she was almost painfully polite, Isa still enjoyed her companionship, and she imagined Lord Kenworth did as well. She decided to sit back and hold her tongue so Lady Sarah and Lady Helen could engage in conversation with Lord Kenworth. They were definitely his best options of those who had been invited to the house party.

Isa noted Lord Kenworth's gaze focused across the path at Lady Phoebe and Lord Thornbrook, who were sitting scandalously close together. And alone. Isa wondered for a moment if he had changed his mind about Lady Phoebe. She was gorgeous, but after her performance last night, was definitely lacking in essentials. Like integrity. She leaned forward over Lord Thornbrook, who was reclining on his back. Considering the cut of her gown, Isa feared he could see all the way to her navel. She drew in a surprised breath, and Lord Kenworth turned to meet her eyes. His raised brow dispelled any doubt she had about his intentions toward Lady Phoebe. Relief flowed through Isa. Of course he would not be fooled by her. With her antics the previous night, she had proven that she wasn't worthy of him.

He leaned close and whispered in her ear, "I bet that was a bit of a shock, even for Thornbrook."

She bit her lip to keep from laughing, and he turned to speak with Lady Sarah. If Isa's life had been different, she could have been one of these ladies enjoying the house party and hoping to find love with one of the many gentlemen present. Though there was no point in dreaming about things that could never happen, she was unable to quell the ache in her heart.

The conversation continued around her, but her mind wandered as she glanced around the property and through the tree line into the woods. She had known that there was a chapel and several other outbuildings usually found on large estates like Walsley, but there were also several large statues sprinkled about as well as what looked like an enclosed pavilion and something that resembled a mausoleum. Though the background of the painting didn't resemble any of these buildings, at least on the outside, there were many excellent hiding places for the tiara at Walsley. Perhaps even an infinite number.

"Miss Winthrop?" Lord Kenworth waved a hand in front of her face.

"Apologies, my lord. I'm afraid I was woolgathering."

"Yes, we can see that. But there is an important matter at hand. We need you to settle a dispute."

She raised her eyebrows and waited for him to continue.

"Lady Sarah has correctly deduced that the color of the pavilion is ochre, and I agree, but Louisa and Lady Helen insist that it is amber."

Isa thought this was quite possibly the most ridiculous argument ever, but she figured it would be impolite to say so. "Actually, I would call it saffron."

Louisa tilted her head and studied the pavilion. "I'm not sure I agree with you. I don't see much of an orange overtone."

"Wait." Lord Kenworth tilted precariously. "When the clouds move in front of the sun, there is more of an orange tone to the color."

"I think you are all ridiculous. The three colors are pretty much the same. Our time would be better served chasing the clouds." Isa stood up and tilted her head back to view the clouds, then spun around like a little girl until she became dizzy and fell on her bottom. She giggled and lay back to watch the sky twirl around her until the dizziness dissipated.

Louisa and Lady Sarah stood and clasped their hands, then whirled around until they fell to the ground like Isa had.

Lord Kenworth raised a questioning brow, but did not join them.

At some point during their silliness, Lady Helen had slipped away. Isa couldn't blame her. They were acting like children, but she didn't regret her behavior. It didn't hurt anyone to have a bit of fun. In a short time she would leave and never see any of them again. She would miss the duchess and Louisa, and even Lord Kenworth. He would always be fixed in her mind with the excitement of searching for the tiara.

Chapter Nine

Edward was surprised to see this playful side of Miss Winthrop when she twirled and dropped to the grass. Her joy was contagious, and she soon had Louisa and Lady Sarah following her. Lady Helen quickly scuttled away. She was a very proper girl, which was to be admired, but she didn't seem to know how to enjoy herself. Perhaps that was why he couldn't drum up any interest in her.

He continued to study Miss Winthrop after she returned to the blanket. She seemed to stay constantly occupied with one task or another. There were times she appeared to carry a heavy weight on her shoulders, and though he knew she was working so she could return to her family, there were certainly worse things than working as a companion to a kind, elderly lady. It made him wonder if there wasn't something else troubling Miss Winthrop. Though her family situation was unfortunate, it wasn't as if serving as a companion was a huge step down for a woman who was not from a noble family. Sometimes even daughters of the nobility were forced to assume a paid position like that of a companion or a governess. Though it reflected poorly on the girl's father, and greatly limited the girl's ability to marry, it wasn't something the girl could control, and sensible people would realize that. Lady Sarah and Lady Helen seemed to accept Miss Winthrop, as did his family. It was only the pretentious among them, like Lady Phoebe and Lady Mary, who seemed put off by her.

Once the twirling ended, the ladies began searching in the grass, and he was puzzled until one of them triumphantly held up a stick. When all three of them had found a stick, Miss Winthrop led them over to the bridge and they tossed their sticks into the creek, then rushed to the other side to see which would appear first. It was a silly game he had played many times as a child, but the ladies were much more civilized than his family had been. There was no arguing or accusations of cheating among them.

The sun emerged from behind a cloud, and for a moment as it moved, it shined on Miss Winthrop only, as if it was trying to draw attention to her. It was a shame that she likely would never have the chance to marry. She might be a bit difficult to manage as a wife, but a man with a strong will who could take charge of her would greatly benefit by an alliance with her. Though she seemed to work hard not to be noticed, if he could determine a way to draw more positive attention to her, she might have a chance at making a good match.

A shadow fell over him, interrupting his thoughts. He shaded his eyes from the sun and looked up. "Thornbrook."

He dropped down next to Edward.

"I see you managed to escape from Lady Phoebe."

"Only just. Imagine what she would be like if her mother weren't here."

"Perish the thought." He considered mentioning her ploy from the previous night, but decided that despite Lady Phoebe's disgraceful behavior, it wouldn't be the gentlemanly thing to do. "I trust you are enjoying yourself now that you no longer fear being devoured."

Thornbrook lay back on the blanket. "I suppose so. I don't mean to disparage your party, but I believe you could have improved upon the guest list."

"Of course I could have, but it was out of my control. My mother chose which ladies to invite."

"That explains it. There are only two, maybe three, ladies of merit here, and at least two of them are off-limits to both of us."

He had to be referring to Louisa and Miss Winthrop. "And if you know what's good for you, you'll stay away from the pair of them."

"I'm not the one who has the problem here. You're the one who has to choose a bride from among them."

Edward lay back next to him. Thornbrook had the right of it. Edward did not want to spend the rest of his life with any of the ladies who attended the party, and he was not going to change his mind in another day, or even a fortnight, so there was no point in continuing this farce.

Unperturbed by Edward's lack of response, Thornbrook continued. "Come on. I think it's obvious to everyone, with the possible exception of you and Miss Winthrop, who has captured your interest."

Edward popped up to a sitting position. "Nonsense. We

are working together only because my mother involved her in the search for a family heirloom. Though I must admit she has proved quite useful in that regard."

Thornbrook shot him an incredulous look. "All right, you've made it clear you don't really want to discuss this. But if you have no interest in any of the ladies present, perhaps you should find an appropriate way to make that known, so the ladies can consider their other options."

Once again, surprisingly, Thornbrook was correct. If there were some way to direct the attention of the ladies to the other men, it would take the pressure off him. The truth was, he wasn't ready to marry anyone. Not until he sorted out his issues with his father and could prove that he was mature enough to be given control of his own estate.

An idea popped into his head that would benefit both he and Miss Winthrop. If Thornbrook was correct, then others must also have noticed Edward spending time with her, and it wouldn't be a complete surprise if he made an offer for her. His mother seemed accepting of her, so she would likely approve, and it would buy him time to show his father that he could be responsible. They would simply have to set an agreed-upon time for her to cry off and, once their engagement ended, her short betrothal to the heir to the Duke of Boulstridge would surely create interest in her from other men. It was the perfect solution. All he had to do was convince Miss Winthrop.

When they returned to the house after the garden tour, the other ladies retired to their rooms to rest before dinner, but Isa went back to the library to take another look at the painting. As soon as she dropped onto the settee, Biscuit jumped into her lap and settled down for a nap. She was going to miss him when they left to return to Concord House.

Though the portrait was already fixed in her mind, she allowed herself to stare at it until her eyes relaxed, hoping she might pick up on a hidden clue or some other hint as to where the tiara was hidden.

She had just decided that it wasn't working when the door swung open and Lord Kenworth came in.

"There you are. I've been looking for you."

Her pulse quickened, and she sat up straight. "You have?"

"Yes." He clasped his hands together, ran his fingers through his hair, then clasped them again. He appeared to be quite agitated.

"Is something amiss, my lord?"

He pushed the door so it was nearly closed, but not latched, then turned back to her. "Miss Winthrop." He swallowed audibly. "Isabella."

She stiffened at the sound of her given name coming from his lips. "Is something wrong? Is it Lady Concord? My brother?"

"No. No, nothing is wrong." He dropped onto the settee next to her. "I'm sorry. I am making a muddle of this."

He raked his fingers through his hair again, leaving it standing up in places. "Since I know you are in need of funds, I have a proposition for you."

Goose pimples instantly formed along her arms, but she did not speak. She cursed the impulse that had motivated her to demand payment for showing them where the painting was. She had hoped he would forget about it when she declined to press him to pay. But George did need the money, and she supposed it was worth misrepresenting herself to help him.

She lifted her eyes and raised her brows, attempting to ignore how warm he was next to her, how a thrill shot through her every time she was alone with him.

"I'm not interested in any of the ladies my parents have invited to the house party, not to mention that I also have no intention of marrying at this point in my life. So, I'd like to pay you to pose as my fiancée."

She leaped off the settee. "No. I could never deceive your parents, and Lady Concord has been so good to me. She would hire a new companion, and then I would be without a job, without a home…"

He stood and clasped her hands. "Calm down, Isabella." He pulled her back onto the settee and massaged the top of her hands in what she was sure would have been a soothing manner had she not been so appalled by his suggestion.

"I'm talking about maintaining our engagement for a few weeks, not months or years. It also has the added bonus of giving us more leeway to be together while we continue our investigation of the tiara. The more time we can devote to it without arousing the undue suspicion of our guests could make the difference between success and failure."

More time to solve the mystery without reproach was welcome, but it still didn't seem right to deceive everyone.

Perhaps sensing her hesitation, he said, "Since I cannot cry off without permanently damaging my reputation, you will have the control to do that whenever you want. I ask only that you wait until after the house party ends."

The warmth from his hands spread through her body, soothing her.

"If you agree, you'll be able to help your brother, and it might even improve your marriage prospects. An engagement to a duke's son will certainly not hurt your chance of making a good match."

Her mind began to work again. There were several benefits to his offer. Not just more time to complete their quest for the tiara but, if he paid her enough, she might be able to move back home. She could help George choose a bride with a nice dowry and get things back on track for both of them. As much as she liked Lady Concord, she yearned to return to her former life, a life where she was once again the daughter of an earl. She might even be able to marry, for he was correct that having been engaged to the heir to a dukedom would give her an entrée back into society.

"What sort of sum are you offering?"

Surprise crossed his face briefly, but she didn't mind, as it suited her purposes for him to think that her only motivation was money.

"What amount are you requesting?"

"One thousand pounds."

His eyes widened. "That amount is larger than many ladies' dowries."

"Don't forget that you still owe me for helping you find the portrait as well."

"Of course. How could I forget that?" He glared at her. "You are a mercenary little thing, aren't you? I'll give you a thousand, but that includes the payment for your help finding the portrait."

It wasn't as much as she had hoped, but it might be

enough to finally get George out of debt. It would have to suffice. "Agreed." She grinned. "Thank you, my lord."

"Since we are now betrothed, you'll have to start calling me Edward. My parents will never believe this engagement is real otherwise."

"Then you should call me Isa. It is how I am known by my family."

"Isa."

It was strange to hear someone use her name after all this time.

"It suits you."

She held out her hand to him, and he rose and clasped it in his warm grip. Her heart flitted around her chest, and she had to catch her breath before speaking. "Are you sure this is what you want? Once you make the announcement, there's no changing your mind."

"I'm certain. Are you?"

She nodded.

"I hope you're as good an actress as you seem to be."

She supposed she deserved that, but it still stung to hear his frank assessment of her.

He walked toward the door, then placed his hand on the latch, but turned back to her before opening it. "Remember, from here on out, you are my betrothed. Considering the exorbitant amount I'm paying you, I expect you to act like it." His stern look was eclipsed by the grin that spread across his face. Perhaps he was also remembering the last time he had said something similar to her. It definitely hadn't turned out as planned.

"Yes, my…Edward." His name felt exciting and even a bit dangerous as it crossed her lips. It would take some time before she would be comfortable using his given name.

When she could no longer hear his footsteps in the corridor, she swept Biscuit off the settee and hugged him to her. "Maybe I'll be able to take you with me after all." And maybe, just maybe, she would finally be able to go home, where she belonged, and help George restore the reputation of their family. Though she hated the need to deceive everyone, surely it was worth a small lie to get back everything she wanted.

Chapter Ten

Once she was dressed for dinner, Isa went to Lady Concord's chamber. She deserved to be the first to know about her engagement to Edward. It pained Isa greatly to have to lie to her, especially since she had been her advocate and the keeper of her true identity for many years. She pressed her hands against her roiling stomach. It could not be helped. Edward had given her an opportunity to help George that she could not refuse. With her resolve firm once again, she knocked on the door.

"Lady Concord?"

"Come in, my dear." She pushed the latch and opened the door. Lady Concord sat in a chair near the fireplace.

"I've barely seen you today. Did you enjoy your tour of the gardens?"

Isa sat in the chair across from her and clenched her hands. "Yes, very much so. The gardens are gorgeous, but I'm sorry I haven't been spending more time with you. I haven't been fulfilling my duties."

"Nonsense. You should be taking advantage of the opportunity to spend time with people your own age."

Isa forced herself to smile. "I came to tell you something. I am betrothed to Lord Kenworth."

Lady Concord took her hand. "My goodness. How did this come about?"

She nearly blurted out that it was a temporary engagement, but though Edward had not asked her to keep the fact that it was not a true betrothal secret, she knew that he expected her to.

"We have spent much time together searching for the missing tiara, and have grown close." Oddly enough, that part was not a lie. As Lady Concord's companion, she had spent very little time with people her own age during the past few years and still felt self-conscious among many of the female guests, but once they had moved past their initial meeting, Isa had grown increasingly comfortable when she was with Edward.

"And he knows who you really are?" Lady Concord raised her brows.

Isa cast her eyes toward the floor.

"Isa, you must tell him immediately."

"I know." She sighed. "I will. But it didn't seem right to tell him moments after he proposed."

"My dear, you cannot build a relationship based on lies. Do not wait too long to confess."

"I won't." Since it wasn't a real engagement, she didn't need to reveal her true identity to him.

Lady Concord stood and opened her arms, and Isa gratefully sank into her hug. "I'm so happy for you, my dear.

I knew it was only a matter of time before some clever young man recognized your merits. "

Isa swallowed down another surge of bile in her throat. She was misleading so many people now it was becoming difficult to keep track. *George*. She had to focus on George and how she would be able to help him. All she had to do was keep anyone from finding out who she was until the house party ended. At most it would be another week, and then she could finally go home.

Though Isa had been uncomfortable telling Lady Concord about her engagement, it had been nothing compared to the uneasiness that swirled in her stomach as she waited to enter the dining room. Louisa and Lady Sarah conversed next to her, and she did her best to smile and nod at the appropriate times, though in truth, she was not following their conversation.

The air around her shifted, and Edward appeared at her side. She breathed in his calming lime and chamomile scent. He leaned close and whispered in her ear, sending shivers up her spine. "My father will announce our betrothal before we go into the dining room."

Isa nodded, and Louisa shot her a smile. Of course she already knew of their engagement. Isa was grateful that Edward's family had accepted her so willingly, but her relief was tainted by guilt at deceiving them all.

The room quieted as the duke and duchess moved toward the entrance to the dining room, then turned to face the assembled guests. "I have an announcement to make. Please excuse the delay while we wait for everyone to receive their champagne," the duke said.

Edward took her arm and led her toward the front of the crowd. Murmurs followed the wake of their path.

"What is he doing escorting that girl? Clearly she does not know her place."

A muscle twitched in Edward's jaw. Isa thought it was Lady Phoebe who spoke, but she couldn't be sure. She wasn't naive enough to expect to be accepted simply because she was engaged to Edward, but she had hoped the rank of his family would at least deter the worst of the gossips.

The duke glanced about the room one more time before speaking. "I am very pleased to announce the betrothal of my son, Lord Kenworth, to Miss Isabella Winthrop."

There was a terrible moment of absolute silence that seemed to last forever, but likely was only a few seconds before Lord Thornbrook said, "Hear, hear."

The duke raised his flute. "To Edward and Isabella."

Isa concentrated on not choking on her gulp of champagne. Though she would have preferred to down the entire flute to take the edge off her nerves, she would behave with perfect decorum so at least no one could fault her manners. Louisa moved to stand next to her, and the guests began to come forward to congratulate them.

Lady Sarah winked at her. "I thought I detected something between you two during the garden tour. Congratulations." Lady Helen was kind as well, but most of the other guests skipped over her and spoke only to Edward. Lady Phoebe and her mother bypassed them altogether. Once all of the guests had the chance to congratulate them, the duke and duchess went into the dining room. Edward took her arm and squeezed her hand before leading her into the room where, for the first time, she was given a seat across from him near the head of the table. Lady Phoebe sat to Edward's left and was careful to avoid making eye contact with Isa. What surprised her the most, though, was that Lady Lydia was sending her venomous looks. Once again, she reminded herself that her situation was temporary, and soon she would be able to go home.

Her Grace had planned for them to play charades after dinner, but everyone was so tired after spending most of the day outside, she decided to put it off for another time. Most of the guests retired early, but Isa was much too wound up to sleep, so she headed for the library.

She wasn't overly surprised to discover Edward and his mother together when she arrived. Edward looked up from the journal and smiled at her as she entered.

"Hello, my dear." Her Grace popped up and squeezed Isa's hand, then performed an exaggerated yawn. "My, it's been a long day. I'll just leave you two to your reading." She grinned at them and hurried from the room.

"Well, that was subtle," Edward said.

Isa sat next to him on the settee. Even though they were close together, but not quite touching, his warmth reached her. Suddenly she felt awkward with him and couldn't think of anything to say. She took a deep breath and reminded herself that their engagement wasn't real.

"Edward."

He glanced up from the journal at the sound of his name.

"Are you finally making progress with the grille?"

He turned to her and met her eyes, and her stomach quivered. Now that there was no longer animosity between them, she allowed herself to admit that he was exceptionally handsome. She nearly reached out to trace the line of his jaw, but instead clasped her hands together on her lap, firmly quelling the urge to discover the texture of his skin.

"I wouldn't call it progress, since I haven't found anything useful, but I have made it most of the way through the journal."

He shifted on the settee, and his arm brushed against her, immediately raising goose flesh on her arm. Good heavens, it had only been the sleeve of his jacket. Why was she so sensitive all of a sudden?

"Are you cold?" He took her hand and rubbed it between his bare hands. His heat easily penetrated her glove. "I'll go stoke the fire."

In fact, she was rapidly becoming overheated, but she could not admit that to him. Being Lady Concord's companion meant that she had not interacted much with men who were close to her own age. Or women, for that matter. Though their alliance was an uneasy one built on a framework of lies and omissions, she had spent more time with him than anyone else, other than her employer, so naturally the relative closeness of their relationship would seem foreign to her. Of course she had cause to be unsettled.

Once the fire was burning bright, he returned to her side. "Is that better?"

"Yes, thank you."

He sat next to her and opened the journal. Isa glanced over and knew immediately which section he was checking.

The passage leaped out at her.

"He took me into his arms and I was awash in exquisite sensation as he showed me the depth of his love."

At first she hadn't understood the passage. In fact, she had thought it a clue until she realized that it was a euphemism for the physical act of love. Edward's focus was on the journal, so she took the opportunity to study him. His long fingers worked gracefully to reposition the grille, and she imagined what it would be like to be held safely in his arms, how easily his gentle touch could make her *"awash in exquisite sensation."* Her heart galloped, and her face immediately filled with heat. She quickly focused her gaze on the floor.

Her movement caught his attention, and she felt his gaze on her, which did nothing to remove the flush from her cheeks.

"Perhaps I've made it too warm in here."

"Not at all." He certainly had, but not in the way he was thinking. Since watching him work was clearly not a good idea, Isa popped up and went to the shelves to search for a book to read. He followed her with his eyes as she sought something that might occupy her mind. Several volumes on the shelves were identical to those that she had once read at her own home. One of the first things she wanted to do once she received the money from Edward was purchase books to refurbish the library at Stowe Hall.

Edward finally returned to his work on the journal, but she kept glancing back at him. Their new agreement had caused her to be much more aware of his presence, the small sounds he made as he read, how the simple act of him being there made the room comfortable and welcoming. She feared it would be more difficult than she had first thought to walk away from him when she cried off. Though it may have been a tactical error for her to accept his proposal, she was hardly in a position to refuse it when it meant she might be able to return to her home and her true identity. She pulled out several books, but none of them piqued her interest.

"Are you having trouble choosing something to read?"

Isa tensed at the soft timbre of his voice. "I suppose I am. Do you have any suggestions?"

The settee squeaked as he stood, and she stiffened when he stopped just behind her.

"Isa, what's wrong? Are you having second thoughts about our arrangement?" He placed his hands on her shoulders and turned her to face him.

"Not exactly. It's just that I hate deceiving your parents and your sister, and Lady Concord."

"As do I, but we are not doing it out of malice." He tucked a stray strand of hair behind her ear and kept his warm hand against her neck.

She feared he could feel the thrum of her pulse reacting to his touch.

"You need to focus on the positive aspects of our situation. You saw the way Lady Phoebe reacted. I am grateful that you are helping me stay out of her clutches. And the other ladies here, the virtuous ones like Lady Sarah, now have a chance to consider the merits of some of the other gentlemen in attendance. That might not have happened if you had not taken me off the market. And, of course, you cannot forget that this is a means for you to help your family."

She nodded. He had made several excellent points, but his hand on her neck and the way he leaned toward her, causing her to mirror his movement, had her quite distracted.

"We will come up with a way to end the engagement that will be amenable to everyone involved."

"How?"

"Well, I'm not sure yet. But we'll think of something."

"Yes, I suppose we will. It's just that there is high risk of something going wrong with our scheme."

His vivid green eyes held her spellbound. She could scarcely think properly.

He slowly removed his hand and took a step back. "Do you want to cry off now? Tell everyone it was a terrible mistake, and you simply cannot wed the horrible Lord Kenworth, even if he will someday inherit a fortune?"

She couldn't help herself. She giggled. "I cannot lie. I would derive great satisfaction from doing that."

"I thought as much."

"Do *you* want to call it off?" She held her breath, afraid to hear his answer.

"No. I would not have suggested it to you if I wasn't certain it would benefit both of us." He cupped her cheek, then ran his fingers over her jaw, and she leaned toward him; she couldn't stop herself.

He met her halfway and pressed his lips softly to hers. A thrill shot through her, and suddenly she needed to be closer to him. She put her hands on his shoulders, and he pulled her against him so they touched from top to bottom. Then his tongue slid across her lower lip, and her knees nearly gave out at the exquisite sensations he evoked.

He pulled back to look into her eyes, and she nearly fell, because she had been leaning against him, and her legs didn't seem to want to support her. She recognized immediately that she was in deep trouble. Whether or not he realized it, he had shown her glimpses of his vulnerable side over the past week. If he had remained arrogant and distant, she might have been able to resist him. But he had let her in just enough to ensnare her, and now she wasn't at all certain she would be able to leave with her heart intact.

Edward hadn't meant to kiss her. It had been longer than he cared to admit since he had kissed someone, but that wasn't why he did it. In truth, he didn't remember making the decision. All of a sudden he just *needed* to kiss her, and he couldn't help himself. He fervently hoped that she was innocent enough not to have recognized the extent of his desire for her.

After taking a step back so he could think clearly, he studied her face. She seemed more dazed than scared, but the primitive part of him was pleased that he had clearly been the first man she had ever kissed. Even an accomplished actress could not have been that convincingly innocent. Though he was certain that there was much more to her than she had as yet revealed, he was confident that he had made the right decision to trust her. Now they could interact with each other freely and once and for all find the tiara. In the excitement of the discovery, it would be easy for her to cry off. She was young and inexperienced, so no one would blame her for changing her mind. And he would play the wounded hero, which should drum up some sympathy for him and would allow him to convince his father to give him more responsibility so he could prove himself.

"I-I should find that book I was looking for," Isa said.

His heart thumped unevenly. *When had he started to think of her as Isa?* He could not allow himself to get too close to her. She was a beautiful temptation, but it would be wrong of him to trifle with her, and he could not marry her. Though his family certainly approved of her, she had not been raised to be the wife of a peer. He couldn't picture her hosting formal dinners or being presented at court. No, they were from two different worlds, and he would do well to remember that.

"Yes, you should. And I need to get back to my deciphering." He picked up the journal and dropped back onto the settee, where he continued his methodical testing of the grille against the pages. He had less than a quarter left and was beginning to think that Isa was correct, and the grille wasn't meant to be used on the journal.

Isa sat next to him with a book, and soon her breathing grew softer and more even. He wasn't surprised to find that she had fallen asleep. He took that as a sign that she was growing more comfortable around him. That was good, because it would make their engagement more convincing, but as he remembered how soft and welcoming her lips were, how charmingly innocent she was, he reminded himself that it would not be prudent for them to become too comfortable with each other. Once he had carefully adjusted her head to rest against his shoulder, he continued with the grille until he had gone through the entire journal. There was no code to be revealed. He sighed at yet another dead end.

Isa began to stir. Her eyes opened, and she blinked. He knew the exact moment when she realized where she was, because she sat bolt upright and stared at him with wide eyes.

He took her hand. "You're fine. You just fell asleep."

"Did I dream…"

"Of my kisses? I imagine so."

"No." She laughed, then glanced at the journal in his lap. "Did you finish?"

He nodded.

She frowned. "You didn't find anything, did you?"

"No, but why did you think that?"

"Because I think the background of the painting is the clue."

He frowned. "Then why would she bother with the grille? To throw us off?"

"I don't think so." Isabella glanced at the books. "I think there's a clue somewhere in the painting that points to one of the books in the library. We just need to find it and figure out which book it is."

He wasn't at all certain she was correct, but it was preferable to another dead end.

She stood and walked over to the shelves where they kept the novels. "You did say that the original books were in the library when your father bought the house, yes?"

"Yes."

"So if we cannot determine which book the picture alludes to, we can simply try all of those that were published during your great-great-grandmother's lifetime."

"Of course, because that will be simple enough."

She placed her hands on her hips. "Do you have any better ideas?"

"No, but perhaps once I've had some sleep I will."

She glanced around, possibly hoping to find a clock

somewhere. "It is late, isn't it?"

"Yes. We should both get some sleep." He tilted his head toward the dog. "Look, even Biscuit has given up."

She giggled. "All right, I suppose we can begin our search for the book tomorrow. Let's go to bed."

He raised a brow. "Together?"

She rolled her eyes at him and picked up Biscuit, cradling him in her arms. For an insane moment, he wished that she would look at him the way she was looking at that dog.

"May I at least walk you to your bedchamber?"

"Yes, I suppose that is permissible. I will need someone to open the door for me so I don't disturb Biscuit."

"I don't think even a gunshot at close range would disturb him." He shoved the grille into the journal and put them both in his pocket. He couldn't hold her hand, since she was cradling Biscuit's limp form in her arms, so he had to content himself with following her down the corridor. Perhaps it was for the best. Though she had warmed to him considerably over the past few days, there was still a part of her that she was holding back, a part of her she didn't seem to wish to share with him. He wanted her more than he ought to, considering that theirs was a temporary business arrangement and could never be more.

Chapter Eleven

The next morning, Isa was plagued with doubt. A strong cup of tea settled her stomach, but nothing could settle her mind. She had finally experienced her first kiss. She pressed her fingertips to her mouth, reliving the gentle touch of his lips on hers, the thrill of his tongue exploring her mouth. Though she would never say so to him, as he hardly needed a boost to his ego, she could admit to herself that Edward was an excellent kisser. Of course, she had no one to compare him with, but somehow she still knew that it had been something out of the ordinary when he kissed her. In any case, it didn't matter because, even if she wanted to marry him, once his family found out she had deceived them, neither he nor his parents would ever trust her again.

Since the excellent weather of the past few days continued, the duke and duchess had invited everyone to play battledore and shuttlecock or archery in the afternoon. Even Lady Concord engaged in a short game with Isabella and Louisa before locating a comfortable seat in the shade from which to watch the activities.

The duke presided over the archery field, observing carefully to ensure no one moved into harm's way. Nearly all the men were occupied with archery, aside from Lord Thornbrook, who seemed content to have the ladies to himself on the battledore and shuttlecock field. It was a simple game, and Isa found it boring for the most part, since there was only so much excitement to be gleaned from batting at a feathered cork to keep it in the air. However, she had decided to avoid the archery field, so there was little else to do. Though she hadn't so much as held a bow in years, she had once been an accomplished archer, and that wasn't the sort of skill most paid companions possessed. Though she no longer worried about being recognized, as several days had passed without incident, her engagement to Edward made it even more imperative that she continue to hide her true identity. It would likely also mean that she could never join London society, since there was a chance that someone from the house party might recognize her, but there was no point in worrying over something she had never had to begin with. Instead, she would focus on the possibility of marrying a country squire who would hopefully make her want to spend all of her days in the country.

"Isabella, do stop staring at Edward and pay attention to the game," Louisa yelled.

Isa supposed she deserved her censure, since she had allowed the shuttlecock to drop twice in a row. "That is an unfair accusation. I don't even know where Edward is."

"Then why do you keep letting the shuttlecock drop?"

"Because I am bored."

Louisa caught it with her hand and walked over to Isa. "Would you rather go to the archery fields?"

"If I did, it would only be to watch."

"Fine. Then you can watch me best our gentlemen players." Louisa winked at Isa and sauntered over to Lord Thornbrook. "My lord, Miss Winthrop has grown bored with our battledore and shuttlecock, and I have promised to provide her with entertainment. I understand that you are an accomplished archer. I should like to offer you a wager."

He tilted his head as he studied her. "What sort of wager?"

"If you win, I will kiss you." His eyes widened, and he opened his mouth as if to speak, but she held up her hand to stop him from interrupting. "And if I win, you owe me twenty pounds."

"Are you certain your father or brother won't kill me?"

She placed a hand on her hip. "Aren't I worth the risk?"

His lips curved into an immense smile. "You just might be."

Louisa turned and jaunted off toward the archery field. Thornbrook followed behind her, his eyes trained on the exaggerated sway of her hips.

Isa had to run to catch up with her. "What are you about?"

She waved her hand in dismissal. "He's done nothing but stare at everyone's breasts all week. I thought it would be fun to humiliate him."

"What if you lose?"

"I won't."

Isa hoped she was correct, because she suspected the duke or Edward *would* kill Thornbrook if Louisa kissed him. She allowed herself to fall back and followed along behind them toward the archery targets.

Edward smiled as she approached. "What's going on with them?" he asked, waving a hand toward his sister and Thornbrook.

"Louisa got tired of him staring at her chest, so she challenged him to a match."

Edward sighed. "I suppose I shouldn't be surprised. Dare I ask what her wager was?"

"If she wins, he owes her twenty pounds."

"And if he wins?"

"She has to kiss him."

Edward grinned. "It's a good thing he won't win. My father would kill him."

"Is she that good?"

He nodded. "It's a bit of family pastime. In fact, you ought to learn, or father will be suspicious."

"Are you offering to teach me?"

"I'd be delighted to teach you." He strolled over to the rack holding the bows.

"Don't you want to watch Louisa first?"

"It would be a waste of time. I have no doubt of the outcome. Thornbrook is doomed."

He picked up one of the bows and tested the string. It was on the tip of her tongue to tell him she preferred a tighter string, but since she was pretending not to know how to shoot an arrow, she would do well to stay quiet.

Isa glanced over at Thornbrook. His first shot landed a good two inches outside of Louisa's, which had hit dead center. His Grace bit back a smile and winked at his daughter.

"Let's head over here, away from the epic duel." Most everyone who was outside was watching Louisa and

Thornbrook.

After placing the arrows on a low table, Edward lifted the bow and turned to her. "Your feet should be shoulder-width apart and at a ninety degree angle to the target."

Isa faced the target and stood as instructed.

"Excellent." Edward came up behind her, wrapped his arms around her, and held the bow where they could both reach it. She sucked in a deep breath and willed herself not to lean back in to him.

"To place the arrow on the bow, hold it horizontally and push the nock onto the string." His lips were next to her ear, and she shivered when his warm breath caressed her. He took her hand in his and guided her through the movements. It was completely unnecessary for him to do that, but she didn't protest.

"Good. Now bring it back to vertical." He helped her rotate the bow, and she closed her eyes for a moment, enjoying the feeling of being held. His cheek brushed against hers, and she caught the faint scent of lime and chamomile.

"Position your index finger above the arrow, and your next two fingers below." He manipulated her fingers into position while she tried to ignore the way his breath teased the sensitive shell of her ear. "The trick is to not grip the arrow, but to just let it rest between your fingers." He jiggled her hand to make sure she wasn't clamping the arrow between her fingers. It was a good thing she already knew how to do this, because Edward's proximity was making it impossible for her to concentrate.

"Now you pull the string." He took his hand from hers and moved back, and she suddenly felt unstable, as if the earth had dropped out from under her.

"Be sure to keep your shoulders straight." He placed his hands on her shoulders. "If you've done everything correctly, your index finger should fit just under your chin."

After a moment he asked, "Are you ready?"

She nodded.

"Then take aim and let it fly."

After a few steadying breaths, she adjusted her aim slightly so the arrow would land to the right, then let go. It hit toward the top of the target.

"Well done." He took her hand and kissed her wrist, just above the edge of her glove, then flicked his tongue over the line of her pulse, sending small jolts of electricity up her arm.

When she recovered from his sensual onslaught, she said, "How is Louisa doing over there?"

"Based on Thornbrook's scowl, I'd say pretty well."

"Have I mentioned how much I like your sister?"

"As long as you like me more, that's just fine."

He came up behind her again, and her pulse quickened in anticipation of his touch.

"This time, be sure to keep the elbow on your bow arm rotated straight up and down." He smoothed his hand over her arm, then she let the arrow go, forgetting to manipulate the shot. The arrow hit dead center.

"Are you sure you haven't done this before?"

She shook her head, not wanting to voice the words that would be a lie. What she needed to do was to find a way to keep his touch from distracting her.

The duke came toward them. "I thought you said she had never used a bow before."

"She hasn't."

"Then either you are an exceptional instructor, or she

has a natural inclination for archery."

"Perhaps it is a bit of both," Isa said, while chastising herself for her lack of concentration. She followed Edward's gaze over to his sister, who had also just sent her last shot dead center on the target. As far as Isa could tell, all of her arrows had landed within inches of the center target. Thornbrook's had not.

He turned to Louisa and bowed. "My lady, I do believe I owe you twenty pounds."

"Yes, you do, my lord."

He placed his hand on her arm, and both Edward and the duke tensed. "I don't suppose you'd still give me that kiss to console me on my humiliating loss?"

For a moment, Isa feared she would slap him, but then she smiled and said, "I'm afraid not. You'll have to find consolation elsewhere."

Edward and his father exchanged a look.

"You wound me, my lady. May I at least escort you back to the house?"

Louisa's eyes narrowed. "If you insist."

He slid his arm through hers, and they began walking.

"That did not end the way I had expected," Edward said.

"No, it certainly didn't." The duke took his leave and followed behind them, his eyes never leaving his daughter.

"It would seem that the afternoon's activities are at an end." Isa glanced around and noticed that only a few of the other guests remained outside. Edward held out his arm to her, and she took it. It was worrisome how easily she was becoming accustomed to his touch, welcoming it, even. She feared how much she would miss it when their temporary arrangement ended.

Lord Thornbrook had cajoled Louisa into reading poetry aloud following dinner. While most of the guests remained in the great hall to listen, Isa left to check on Lady Concord, then went to the library, where she once again sat and stared at the painting. There was a clue she was missing. There had to be.

Perhaps she was going about this the wrong way. Instead of looking to the painting for the clue, she would search the books. Though she could be wrong, instinct told her that the answer lay in one of the books that had been in the library when the tiara was hidden. With no better options available, she decided to focus on the novels.

It wasn't as difficult as she thought it would be. Though she hadn't thought ahead to get the grille from Edward, there were limited numbers of novels that dated from the eighteenth century, and of those, several were too small to accommodate the grille. She had narrowed it down to only sixteen books when she stumbled upon a book with a picture on the title page that exactly matched the background of the portrait.

Isa jumped up. She had to find Edward and get the grille. She turned toward the door and nearly collided with him.

"If I had known you would be so excited to see me, I would have sought you out earlier."

She smiled up at him. "I found it."

His eyes widened. "Found what?"

"The book." She held it out so he could see the picture. "Do you have the grille?"

He pulled the journal from inside his coat and handed her the grille. "I guess I should have listened more closely when you said the picture was from a novel."

"Yes, well. It was just a theory that happened to be correct." She rushed back and settled herself on the settee. Edward plunked down beside her. It didn't require much thought to apply the grille to the pages to determine if the words revealed created a legible sentence, but Edward's intense scrutiny distracted her nonetheless.

"Don't you have anything better to do than stare at me?" she asked.

"Not particularly, though I suppose I could find something else to occupy myself."

"Thank you." She returned her focus to the book, but nearly dropped it when Edward ran his finger over the outside of her ear. "What are you doing?"

"Occupying myself." His finger continued down her ear, along her jawline, and then down into the hollow above her collarbone.

"That is not helping my concentration." It was, however, making her pulse thrum.

"Good."

She cast her eyes toward the ceiling. "If I cannot focus, I won't be able to find the next clue."

"But the texture of your skin is so tempting."

She dropped the book into her lap and turned toward him. "I cannot think when you're touching me." He was likely just teasing her, but she was in real danger of succumbing to him if she didn't make him stop. Normally she was invisible, but he was the first person, the only person, who had noticed her as a woman. Her body tingled, aching for more of his touch.

He held out his hands, palms up. "Fine. I'll leave you alone. But don't think I haven't filed that information away for later."

His statement raised equal parts excitement and trepidation that rushed through her as if they had been pumped out by her heart.

He left the settee and stood studying the painting.

Isa turned back to the book, mostly relieved that he had left and, six pages later, she found it.

"This is it!" She read the words to him. "*Where the green cloak grows, light permeates the dark and deep*."

"Excellent. Another obscure clue." Edward sighed. "I'm beginning to think the tiara is long gone, and we're on a wild-goose chase."

"Maybe not." Isa stood and paced in front of the fireplace. "'*Where the green cloak grows*.' That must be a reference to plant life of some sort. Is there an outbuilding at Walsley surrounded by dense foliage?"

Edward ran his fingers through his hair. "Not that I know of. And if the clue does refer to foliage, it could be wildly different from what it was at the time the clue was written."

"Perhaps, but maybe she thought of that. Maybe there's a place that hasn't changed all that much through the years. It could be part of a garden that she assumed would be maintained."

He shook his head. "The problem is that the entire estate was left unattended from the time my grandmother left until father purchased it more than two decades later. It fell into disrepair, so changes that she could not have anticipated may have been made."

"So are we going to give up?"

"Of course not. We'll just have to go exploring tomorrow. Mother had planned for everyone to perform a play, so I think we'll have to sneak out while they're rehearsing. If we go on horseback it will shorten the amount of time we're gone."

"Don't you think we, or at least you, will be missed?"

"Let me go talk to Mother. We need to share the clue with her anyway, and she might remember something I've forgotten. I'm certain she knows a way to conceal our absence so we're not missed."

"Who will serve as my chaperone?" As much as she would enjoy an afternoon alone with Edward, she had to think of her future.

He took a step closer to her, so close that she caught a whiff of chamomile, and immediately warmed from the heat emanating from him. "Are you afraid to be alone with me? After all, as you keep reminding me, this is a sham engagement."

"I'm alone with you now, aren't I?" She raised a brow at him. "You know it's not that, but I must have care for my reputation. When I cry off, I need to leave with my respectability intact. Being alone inside a house full of other people is different than riding out alone to unknown locations."

Edward closed his eyes and rubbed his forehead. "I'm sure Louisa, or perhaps my mother or father, would be happy to accompany us. We may have to wait another day or two, but I'll see what I can arrange."

"Thank you."

The room seemed less cozy once Edward left. After wrapping her shawl around her shoulders to ward off the chill, she made herself comfortable on the settee. In addition to her reputation, she would do well to remember to protect her heart. Though their initial meeting had not gone well, Edward had proved to be worthy of her regard. Given their wealth and position in society, the entire family was admirable, and Isa would regret having to leave them. Though she felt remorse for deceiving them with their temporary engagement, she understood why Edward felt it was his best option. Lady Phoebe's attempt to compromise herself came to her mind and reminded her that he also benefited from their arrangement. She would leave, and they would eventually forgive him, and she could only hope it wouldn't be too painful for her when their arrangement came to its inevitable end.

Since she was too unsettled to sleep, Isa decided to continue applying the grille to the pages of the novel. There was always the possibility that the book contained more than one clue and, if nothing else, it would take her mind off her growing attraction to Edward, because to let it deepen was as harrowing as the possibility of never seeing him again after she left Walsley.

Chapter Twelve

It would be difficult for Edward to be less pleased with the arrangements that had been made. Mother agreed wholeheartedly with Isa that, given the number of people staying at the house, they could not explore the grounds without a chaperone. Louisa had volunteered to accompany them, and somehow Thornbrook had managed to secure an invitation as well. Now, instead of being alone with Isa, or even having time to focus on finding the next clue, Edward would have to keep an eye on Thornbrook to make sure he behaved appropriately toward both his sister and Isa.

Thornbrook and Louisa had already mounted and were letting their horses amble around the lawn while they waited for Isa. At long last, Edward spotted her on the path to the stables and waved to the grooms to bring out their horses.

After a quick stop to speak with Louisa, she finally made her way over to him, looking radiant in her dark blue riding habit and a hat that resembled a man's top hat, except that it was made feminine by virtue of its soft velvet fabric. Her eyes reflected the color of the cloudless sky, and his breath caught when she turned her radiant smile on him.

"My apologies for delaying our departure. Biscuit was very insistent about joining us. Her Grace finally closeted him in her sitting room, where he will hopefully remain for the duration of our ride."

Waving away the groom, Edward helped her mount and made certain his hand slid over the curve of her hip and along the length of her thigh. For one wild moment, he considered galloping off with her into the woods where he could take her to one of the lesser-known outbuildings at Walsley and spend the rest of the day exploring every last bit of her.

Instead, he said, "You are so captivating, I'm willing to forgive your tardiness."

After mounting his own horse, he threw a scowl toward Thornbrook. The man had been spending far too much time chasing after Louisa. When the ladies moved away, Edward decided it was time to warn him off, since he was ignoring the unwritten gentlemen's code that should have kept him away from a friend's sister.

Edward squeezed his horse into a trot and rode up next to him. "Why are you here?"

"In England?"

He narrowed his eyes. "Why are you here, on a horse, instead of inside memorizing your part for the play?"

"Because it is a beautiful day to be outside enjoying fine weather and equally fine company. Well, aside from you."

"Thornbrook, what are you doing sniffing around my sister?"

"I enjoy her company."

"You enjoy the hunt. She's the first woman who has not only bested you, but turned you down."

Thornbrook shrugged. "I admit she has proved to be more of a challenge than most ladies, but—"

"There are no buts. She is my sister, and you need to stay away from her."

"I have no intention of dishonoring your sister. I just enjoy her company. It's refreshing to be around a woman who has no interest in my title or inheritance. Or me, for that matter."

Good lord. Thornbrook sounded just like him when he tried to convince himself that he had suggested a false engagement to Isa for the same reasons. He was in trouble on both counts.

"If I catch you so much as looking at her the wrong way—"

Thornbrook held up a hand. "I know."

For now, Edward needed to focus on finding the bloody tiara. There would be time later to sort out everything else. He loosened the reins, and his stallion soon caught up with the ladies.

"So what, exactly, are we looking for out here?" Louisa asked.

"A place that fits this description, '*Where the green cloak grows, light permeates the dark and deep*'," Isa said. "We assumed it had to refer to vegetation of some sort."

Louisa sighed. "This is going to be a challenge. There are many, many places at Walsley that were allowed to become overgrown prior to Papa purchasing the property."

Thornbrook used his hand to shade his eyes and looked at Edward. "It would probably be best if we started at the far corner of the property and worked our way back toward the house."

Edward nodded and gestured for the ladies to take the lead.

"How old was your great-great-grandmother when she hid the tiara?" Isa asked.

That was a non sequitur. Edward narrowed his eyes at her. "I'm not certain. Probably in her fifties. Why?"

"It seems to me that a lady would not traverse the wild areas of the estate in order to hide the tiara, and it seems equally likely that she would leave it in at least a somewhat sheltered space to protect it."

"Perhaps, though there was no reason for her to suspect that it would remain hidden for so long. She had no way of knowing that the property would ever pass from the family." He glanced down the line where the manicured lawn met the edge of the woods. "So you're saying that we should narrow our search to places closer to the house where there may have been a sheltered hiding place."

"And, we can rule out all of the manicured areas we're familiar with," Louisa said. "So it seems that we've limited ourselves to the space outside of the gardens, formal areas, and the planted fields, but not into the places that have always been wild."

Edward waved a hand to his left. "Then let's traverse the border behind the gardens and see what we find." Clucking to his stallion, he took off at a brisk canter toward the edge of the woods. Thornbrook came up beside him, and Edward gave his horse his head. Both horses surged forward and they raced to the tree line. After pulling up his horse and giving him a pat on the neck, he glanced around and found that Isa and his sister were walking along the edge of the forest, occasionally pushing or pulling vines and branches out to view what lay behind them.

Edward pulled out his handkerchief to wipe his brow, then rode up alongside Isa. "Have you spotted anything interesting yet?"

"I've discovered the true meaning of 'green cloak.'" She sighed. "The vines make it difficult to see much. It doesn't seem likely that there's anything to be found back here. I don't suppose you have an old map of the property somewhere?"

"I'm afraid not. I already spoke with my father. He had the land surveyed after he purchased the estate, but there aren't any maps or diagrams that would tell us how it looked before it fell into disrepair, and of course, any paintings that might have been of use were either taken from the house or sold." He reached over and pulled a bit of vine off Isa's hat and allowed his fingers to trail down her neck. Her shiver pleased him more than it ought to. He couldn't seem to keep his hands away from her, but he needed to back off before he scared her. He could also use a reminder that they had agreed only to a temporary arrangement, which meant that he could not allow things to go any further, no matter how much he wanted them to.

Louisa and Thornbrook had fallen behind them. Her laugh punctuated the air, and Edward turned back to give Thornbrook a warning look.

"Do you really think the tiara is still here? Could it survive outside for all of these years?"

He shook his head. "I don't know. Maybe the tiara isn't out here, and the clues will just lead us to yet another clue."

They continued following the edge of the forest until

they reached the halfway point where they were parallel to the house. It was already late afternoon, and Edward feared they would fail to make any progress before it became too dark to continue. The sky had darkened with cloud cover, and rain couldn't be too far off.

"Edward, look." Isa unhooked her leg from between the pommels of her sidesaddle and jumped off her horse, exhibiting skills that seemed advanced for an impoverished country squire's daughter who now worked as a companion.

"I thought you said Lady Concord no longer rides."

"She doesn't, but when I first began working for her, we rode every day." Without further conversation, Isa tossed the reins of her horse to Edward and plunged through the brush into the woods.

"Isa, wait." He scrambled from his horse and whistled loudly. Louisa heard him and turned her mare toward them. It seemed to take an interminably long time for her to get there. All of their horses were trained to ground tie, but a stray clap of thunder could leave them with a long, wet walk back to the house, and he didn't quite trust his stallion with the mare he had given Isa, who happened to belong to his mother.

Louisa arrived with Thornbrook on her heels. "Have you found something?"

"I'm not sure, but Isa is already scavenging through the woods. I need you two to stay with the horses." Without waiting for them to dismount, he turned and plunged after Isa.

After a frantic search that seemed to take forever, but probably lasted only seconds, he spotted Isa about a hundred meters away.

"Isa, you mustn't run off like that. Do you have any idea how quickly you can become lost out here?"

"Not that quickly," she replied over her shoulder. "Look. Boxwood."

"There's boxwood growing wild all over England."

She lifted a hand and waved him forward. "They're planted in a specific pattern. They're not wild." With her glove brushing against the leaves, she followed the line of the bushes.

"Those were planted a long time ago. There must have been a garden here at one time." He followed behind her as the line of remarkably tall boxwood—they had to have been at least twenty-five feet high—curved to the right. A huge gust of cold air rattled the branches of the trees above them, reminding him that rain was imminent.

He opened his mouth to suggest that they come back tomorrow when they had more time to explore, but Isa was nowhere to be found. He charged forward and spotted her through an overgrown opening in the bushes.

She grinned at him. "I think it's a maze. See how it continues to curve around, and there's another opening."

"It's a huge maze." He glanced up at the dark sky just as the first raindrop hit his cheek. "Isa, we shouldn't go any farther. We need to get back before we are soaked by the rain, and it isn't safe to explore the maze without letting my mother and father know what we're doing. If we became lost, no one would know where to look for us." And he would once again be labeled irresponsible.

She frowned and moved to stand in front of him. "I know. It would be all too easy to get lost in any maze, let alone one as unkempt as this." She made some sort of growling sound and stomped her foot. "But we're so close."

Maddeningly close. "We'll come back tomorrow morning, armed with sustenance and hedge clippers."

She laughed and placed her glove against his cheek. It was all the invitation he needed. He pulled her to him and kissed her. When he ran his tongue across the seam of her lips, her mouth opened in an invitation he didn't waste any time accepting.

"Ahem."

Edward registered the sound of someone clearing his throat. He placed one last kiss against Isa's lips and glanced over his shoulder.

"Sorry to interrupt," Thornbrook said, "but all hell is about to break loose over our heads."

Edward and Isa both looked up just as the first boom of thunder rumbled over them. He took her hand and dashed back with her through the opening in the boxwood, heading for the tiny bit of light that signaled the edge of the field.

"Had I known you were merely looking for some privacy, I would have come to fetch you sooner," Thornbrook quipped.

Louisa sighed with relief when they emerged. "Thank goodness. I wasn't sure how I was going to make it back to the house leading four horses."

"My apologies, Louisa. But I think we found it," Isa said.

Louisa's brows drew together. "Found what?"

"The hiding place. The place the clue referenced. There's an old, overgrown maze back there."

Louisa grinned. "I can't believe this is happening. After all this time. Mother will be ecstatic."

"Yes, well, if you'd like to survive to tell her about it,

we need to get going right now." Thornbrook tossed Louisa onto her mare and quickly pulled himself onto his gelding.

Edward glanced over his shoulder at the sheet of rain that was heading straight for them. Grabbing Isa around her middle, he placed her in the saddle and handed her the reins then mounted his stallion. They took off at a gallop but were too slow to avoid the rain. By the time they reached the house, Edward was soaked through. He rode straight into the covered area of the lower courtyard, and the others followed him. Once a groom arrived to take the horses, they entered through the kitchens.

"Mrs. West. Can you please arrange for baths to be prepared immediately for both Lady Louisa and Miss Winthrop?"

"Of course, my lord. You poor dears." She turned and rushed off to find the housekeeper, muttering on her way out, "You'll all catch your death if you don't get out of those wet clothes."

One of the maids rushed over and handed them lengths of toweling to dry off.

"Thank you," Edward said. After turning toward Isa and noting her shiver, he wrapped his toweling around her and lifted her into his arms. "Your lips are tinged blue. Let's get you up to your chamber."

"Edward, put me down. I can walk myself."

"I'll get you there faster." Taking the steps two at a time, he rushed up the servants' staircase, taking care to hold her tight so he didn't jostle her too much. He slowed slightly going down the corridor, then shoved in through her door, where the maids were busy filling a tub with hot water.

He gently dropped her to her feet and placed a kiss against her forehead. "Go get those wet clothes off immediately. You can wrap yourself in a blanket until your bath is ready."

"I'm not a child. I'll be fine."

"Then do as I say or I'll undress you myself." He crossed his arms.

She giggled and pushed him toward the door. "I will as soon as you leave."

"I'm not leaving until I know—"

"Get out!"

With more strength than he would have expected from her, she shoved him through the door and slammed it closed behind him.

"I'll be back soon to make sure you followed my orders."

A large, heavy object slammed into the door, rattling it against the frame.

He whistled as he moved down the corridor.

Chapter Thirteen

Isa read the same line of *Oliver Twist* for the fifth time. Biscuit, who was trying to sleep next to her, sighed. After her bath she didn't have the energy to dress for dinner, let alone stay awake through several removes, so she had asked for a light repast to be brought to her room. Whenever the slightest sound slipped under her door, her stomach jumped. A part of her feared the implications of a return visit from Edward, but the rest of her, the much larger part, waited in anticipation. Over the last few days, their relationship had grown and changed from friendship into something more, but whether that meant anything with respect to their arrangement was still to be determined. It seemed impossible that he would ever be able to forgive her for deceiving him about who she was. If there was to be any chance that they could make their engagement real, she had to find a way to make him understand why she hadn't told him sooner.

A knock sounded on the door and she leaped out of the

bed, straightening her dressing gown as she moved toward the door. After taking a deep breath, she pulled the door open. Apparently determining that Edward was not a threat, Biscuit positioned himself back in the middle of her bed.

He glanced up and down the corridor before slipping in and leaning against the door. His eyes widened as they swept over her dressing gown and up to her loose hair. "I shouldn't be in here," he said in soft tones, "but I had to make sure myself that you're all right."

"A little summer rain never hurt anyone." Suddenly feeling shy, she added, "And this dressing gown covers more of me than any of my gowns you've already seen me in."

He swallowed audibly. "I wanted to thank you for your help with our treasure hunt. My mother is so excited I doubt she'll sleep at all tonight." He took a step closer and cradled her cheek. "None of this would have happened without you."

"I assure you it was simply a matter of luck that turned out to be fortuitous for all of us."

He smoothed her hair, then took her hand and placed a kiss on her palm. "I should go before someone catches me in here."

"I can assure you I don't have any regular nighttime visitors."

"I should hope not. Nevertheless, it isn't proper for me to be here, as much as I'd like to stay."

A sudden fear that she would never have another chance like this with him sent shards of ice through her veins, and an involuntary shiver overtook her. He was the only one who had been able to see past her position as a companion and accept her as she was. She had become closer to him than she was to any other person, and she would not squander the opportunity to be with him. He was worth the risk, worth taking a chance that their relationship might turn into something more. "Will you stay?"

"I shouldn't, and yet, I can't resist you."

Isa didn't know exactly what she was asking of him, but she knew she needed him with her, holding her, comforting her. His mere touch soothed her, assuaged her fears, made her believe in a future she had never imagined possible until she met him.

She took his hand and led him toward her bed.

"Isa. I can't…I won't…"

"Shh." She pressed a finger to his lips. "Right now, I just need you to hold me."

Pulling him toward the bed, she shoved Biscuit to the far side, tossed the covers back, and slipped in, dragging him along with her.

"Isa."

She couldn't bear to meet his eyes. "If this isn't what you want, just go. Now, before I die of shame."

He put two fingers under her chin and forced her to look at him. "Isa, what I want, and what I should do, are two very different things."

His eyes held hers.

"Do what you *want* with me."

His breath ragged, he pulled her to him. Her head fit perfectly under his chin, and his warmth surrounded her. It had been so long since anyone had held her she had forgotten what it felt like to feel safe, feel wanted.

She held her breath as he nuzzled her hair, then placed her palm flat against his chest, comforted by the strength of his steady heartbeat. The faint scent of lime tickled her nose, awaking desire in her. She slid herself up his body and loosened the buttons at the top of his shirt so she could explore the planes of his chest.

He groaned and grabbed her hand. "Isa, I can't… If you keep touching me, I won't be able to stop myself. I want you, but—"

She kissed him, silencing his protests with action. Sliding her fingers through his hair, she held him to her, and she pushed her tongue into his mouth just as he had done to her earlier. He groaned, and it encouraged her to keep going. She pulled his shirt from his waist and touched her fingers to the hard planes of his warm stomach, then slid down his body so she could kiss his smooth skin. The contrast of silky skin and crisp hair tickled her lips and sent pulses of need through her.

All of a sudden she was lifted up and flipped onto her back. Biscuit yipped and jumped off the bed. Edward rose up and for one horrible second she thought he was going to leave, but he simply pulled his shirt over his head and tossed it onto the floor then reached for the ties of her dressing gown. Once he had opened it, he ran a finger down the length of her collarbone, then over the taut peak of her raised nipple. She arched her back, wanting more, wanting to feel the heat of his bare skin against hers. Taking her cue from him, she divested herself of her dressing gown and pulled her night rail off over her head. Goose pimples immediately formed on her skin, and the cool shock of the sheets made her shiver. She had no idea where her boldness was coming from, but even with her inexperience, she recognized that what was between them was special, and she would never find it again with someone else. She was willing to take the risk, because being with him once was better than never feeling this way.

Not wasting a second, Edward bolted off the bed, removed what was left of his clothing in one fluid movement, and returned to her. As his gaze roamed over her body, she closed her eyes and wished she had doused the lamps, though the fireplace provided ample light as well.

"Isa, open your eyes."

She shook her head.

He flipped her hand over and kissed the inside of her wrist, her palm. "Dearest, look at me."

She gulped and opened her eyes.

"Do you trust me?"

She nodded.

"Then let me love you properly. No fear. No regrets."

"No regrets."

He sealed their agreement with a devouring kiss to her lips. His hand moved down her arm in a reassuring caress that continued over her hip. He pulled back to meet her eyes, then ran his hand up her side. The pad of his thumb flitted over her nipple, generating an answering response between her legs. She raked her nails down his chest then pulled him closer. He kissed down her neck and along her collarbone, then slid farther down and applied his tongue to her breast. Her hips lifted off the bed as his tongue circled her nipple then pulled it into the wet heat of his mouth and laved it with his tongue until she cried out.

Before she could recover, his hand slid down and cupped the apex of her thighs. She closed her eyes, embarrassed by the wetness between her legs.

"Isa, look at me."

She shook her head and kept her eyes firmly closed.

Heat suffused her face and neck.

"You needn't feel ashamed. This is what is supposed to happen between us. It lets me know that you want me as much as I want you."

Pressing his warm hand against her stomach, he held her in place as he slid down and kissed the insides of her thighs. She tensed, and he caressed the soft skin with his lips until she relaxed again. Then his tongue stroked the place between her legs, igniting a flame in her. She moaned, and he began moving more quickly, pressing his tongue hard against that fiery place, then teasing her with gentle licks before pressing harder again. Something was building within her. Something new and stunning that sparked inside her like a flame. He increased the pressure, giving her impossible pleasure before she finally exploded into ecstasy.

Before her breath slowed, he slid back up her torso and used his wicked tongue to stimulate her nipple. She moaned in pleasure and shoved her hands into his hair, holding his mouth firmly to her breast. The place between her legs throbbed, and she took his hand and pushed it toward that spot. Her need temporarily overwhelmed her embarrassment. He obliged instantly, pressing his thumb down hard on that most sensitive place and gently pushing one of his fingers up inside her. His thumb assaulted her while his finger moved gently inside, and she came apart again.

He glided up her body and kissed her. She opened her mouth and slid her tongue into his mouth to explore. The evidence of his desire for her pressed against her thighs, and she reached down and tentatively stroked him, then pushed him toward her opening. It was half agony, half ecstasy to have the soft skin of his manhood brush against her, and she lifted her hips, inviting him to slide into her.

"Are you certain this is what you want, Isa?"

She responded by grasping his hips and yanking him toward her. He entered her slowly, driving her wild until he hit a barrier and a hint of pain shot through her. "I think you're too big."

He laughed. "No, dearest. You are too small. We need to take this slowly to minimize the pain, but I'm afraid it's still going to hurt the first time."

The fact that he said first time implied that there would be a second time, which made her desire him even more desperately. Even if it was painful, she wanted him inside her, filling her up, making her feel whole at least for a little while.

"If it's going to hurt, then it's better to go fast. I don't care if it hurts as long as you are able to feel the same things I've been feeling."

He broke through the barrier in one thrust, and at first it hurt like nothing she had ever experienced, a searing pain that stole her breath. She didn't allow herself to cry out, and a moment later, his warmth and assurance filled her. When he began to slowly move back and forth, the fire sparked again. He leaned down to kiss her, and his tongue moved to the rhythm of his thrusts. Moments later, they both exploded, and Isa's last thought before she succumbed to exhaustion was to hope that the fieriness of their connection would fuse their souls together forever.

When Isa's breaths became rhythmic with sleep, Edward eased himself off of her and rolled onto his side, then pulled her tight against him and tucked the covers around them. It was still full dark outside, so he had time before he needed to leave her to sneak back to his own chamber. She had nearly stopped his heart when she had said she didn't mind pain as long as he could feel the same thing she did. No one else he had been with had ever given a thought to his welfare. She had a way of reaching inside to see who he really was, which both excited and terrified him. His wealth and status wasn't what had attracted her to him. Given the way he had acted when they first met, she had viewed it as a detraction. She hadn't begun to warm up to him until he relaxed around her and revealed who he really was. With her, he wasn't the idle, freeloading son of a duke who had everything but valued nothing. Instead, for the first time, her regard made him want to be better, to do more. She challenged him, exasperated him, and tempted him in a way that no other woman ever had, and she had him thinking that the best thing for both of them would be to make their engagement real.

Chapter Fourteen

It was the warmth of the sun contrasting with the cool sheets and not the light that eventually woke Isa. She glanced around, hoping Edward might still be there, but of course he was not. It wouldn't do to have anyone see him leaving her chamber in the bright morning sunlight. A lengthy stretch allowed her to catalogue the places that had stiffened during the night, but most of all, she was overwhelmingly content, despite the fact that she had taken a huge risk in being intimate with Edward. The chance to be with him, to experience true pleasure and happiness with someone she cared about at least once in her life, was worth any risk. She had no doubt that he was an honorable man and would take care of her in the event that a child should come as a result of her actions, but most of all she hoped that as they continued to grow closer to each other, she could find a way to make him understand why she had had to assume a false identity. This could finally be her chance to be happy, and she was going to do everything she could to make it happen.

She had slept much later than usual and someone had already taken Biscuit outside. She experienced a pang of guilt that she had barely seen Lady Concord over the past few days. Of course, once their engagement had been announced, no one expected Isa to continue as Lady Concord's companion, but she still enjoyed her company. She would be sure to visit with her that evening, after they had explored the maze and hopefully found the tiara. Excitement swelled within her at the thought of spending the day with Edward, and she dressed quickly and hurried down the staircase just in time to spot him exiting the house.

"Isabella, do come eat something before we leave." Louisa waved her into the breakfast room.

"Edward is gathering supplies so we can be prepared to explore the maze."

Isa nodded and moved to the sideboard where the food was laid out. She selected a few slices of bacon and some toast and strawberry jam, and what turned out to be dried trout, which she would not be eating as she was not fond of fish. She really ought to pay more attention to what she was doing, but her mind was refusing to focus. After choosing a seat across from Louisa, she prepared her tea and started eating without paying much attention to the food.

"Mother is quite adamant that we take four servants with us. A footman to enter the maze with us, two grooms to manage our equipment and take care of the horses while we are within the maze, and a second footman to send for help if we get lost." She frowned. "As I'm sure you can imagine, Edward and Thornbrook are not best pleased with the arrangements."

"I'm surprised Her Grace is not joining us as well."

"Oh, she wants to, but Father insisted that she had to remain to entertain our guests. He tried to make me stay as well, but Edward argued that you had to go to help decipher any clues we might find, and of course you cannot go without another female present." Louisa ate more bacon. "It's not as if this is my house party. If anyone has to stay behind, it should be Edward. Of course, now that you two are engaged, the purpose of the house party has been fulfilled, so I suppose my father is correct that he and Mother must remain to entertain our guests."

Isa could barely follow Louisa's dizzying explanation, perhaps because she kept listening for the sound of Edward's footsteps in the corridor. She swallowed the last of her tea and stood. "Are you ready?"

"I've been ready for more than an hour, but Edward demanded that we not wake you."

A thrill shot through Isa. Though she was unused to having anyone worry about her needs, she found it to be quite heartening. "I'm sorry to have slowed down the preparations. In the future, do feel free to ignore him."

"They are still making their arrangements, so you weren't really holding us up anyway."

Her Grace appeared in the doorway. "Louisa, may I speak with you for a moment?"

She wiped her mouth and stood. "Of course. Please excuse us, Isabella."

Isa sat down and refilled her tea. Footsteps sounded outside the door moments later, and Thornbrook entered.

"Good morning. May I join you?"

"Of course, my lord."

He sat next to her. "I've already eaten, but I saw you sitting here alone as I was passing by. I thought perhaps you could use some company."

"Thank you for your consideration, my lord, but Lady Louisa was called out for a moment. I believe she will return shortly."

"Then we have no time to waste."

"I'm sorry?" Isa said, wondering what he was about.

He leaned closer to her and lowered his voice. "I need your help. I find myself rather infatuated with Lady Louisa, but I don't know how to get her attention."

Isa nodded. "I can see how that would be an uphill battle for you. You might try simply behaving like a gentleman."

"That's not as easy as it sounds."

"Yes, well, I'm certain if you apply yourself, the abrupt change in your demeanor will attract her notice."

"Are you implying that I do not generally behave as a gentleman?"

"Even now, your gaze is a bit south of my eyes, is it not?"

His face colored and Isa nearly laughed. "You see my point."

He nodded.

"Am I interrupting something?" a voice edged with steel said from the doorway.

Thornbrook snapped away from her, and Isa turned to look over her shoulder. Edward glared at them both, but surely he knew this was none of her doing.

Louisa strode up and stopped next to Edward.

"Thornbrook, I could use your help with the equipment. We'll meet you outside shortly," he said to Louisa, then left without addressing Isa.

"Do you think he is upset with me?" she asked Louisa.

"I suspect he's jealous. Once his brain starts to function again, he'll realize that it was all Thornbrook's doing. He's such a flirt. I wouldn't be surprised if he did it just to get a rise out of Edward."

They left the breakfast room, and Isa followed Louisa up and down several staircases and through multiple corridors before they stepped into the courtyard between the house and the stables. She adjusted her bonnet and waited impatiently for the horses to be brought out. Did Edward regret what had transpired between them, or was Louisa correct that he was simply jealous? She had so been looking forward to spending the day with him and learning more about him. Even if he was having second thoughts, she had no regrets about giving herself to him. It was worth it to have the memory of that night to carry with her forever.

Finally, a groom led their horses from the stables and helped Isa and Louisa to mount. Letting the horses have their heads, they ambled along the paths through the gardens. At long last, Isa spotted Edward coming toward them on his stallion, with Thornbrook and the grooms following along behind.

"Good morning. Are you ladies ready to explore the maze?"

Isa nodded, suddenly feeling an unexpected shyness with Edward.

Louisa glared at him. "What took so long? We could have left more than an hour ago."

"Mother. She insisted on helping to collect the supplies we would need, including food, lanterns to navigate the maze, and a myriad of other things we now have to haul along with us. We have provisions for at least a week should we need them."

"That sounds about right," Louisa mumbled.

The sound of large items banging together reached her ears, and Isa glanced behind her to find two grooms driving a large cart full of supplies. She bit her lip to keep from laughing at Edward's exasperated expression, but she couldn't prevent the smile from forming on her lips.

"Not a word from you," he whispered as he drew up beside her. "I thought we would never be able to leave. As it is, we may run out of daylight before we're able to make our way through the maze."

She giggled, but then he turned to her with a serious expression. "What happened with Thornbrook in the breakfast room?"

"I'm not sure. I think he's feeling a bit lonely. Most of the mothers are not allowing him near their daughters." Isa didn't think it would be wise to tell Edward that Thornbrook was in love with his sister.

"Maybe, but that's never stopped him before. I'll speak with him about it later."

Isa breathed a sigh of relief. It appeared that Edward had simply been jealous.

Yesterday, Edward had tied his handkerchief to the fence to mark the location where they needed to enter the woods to reach the maze, and Thornbrook's cloth marked the boxwood that led into the maze.

Once they were far enough from the house, they allowed the horses to maintain a slow canter, not wanting to get too far out in front of the wagon. When they reached the first handkerchief, Edward jumped off his horse and handed him to a groom, then lifted Isa from her horse and slid her down his body, reigniting her desire for him instantly, even through all of their layers of clothing. He lifted her hand and kissed it, then turned to gather equipment from the cart.

Disappointment skittered through her, but she supposed he was trying not to do anything that might arouse suspicions about what had transpired between them last night.

Louisa looped her arm through Isa's, and they stepped into the maze. "What are we looking for?"

Isa recited the clue again. "*Where the green cloak grows, light permeates the dark and deep.*"

"So some sort of plant that grows over something dark and deep." She nodded. "That won't be at all difficult to find."

Isa laughed at her strained expression. "We cannot count on the clue being what we think it will be. The green cloak might be the boxwoods, in which case, all we need to find is the dark, deep place within."

"Are you talking about Thornbrook again?" Edward quipped.

Isa glared at him and continued. "There ought to be plenty of dark places inside the maze. But, of course, with it being so overgrown…"

"Not so fast, ladies." Thornbrook drew up behind them. "We must stay together so no one gets lost in the maze."

"He is correct," said Edward. He handed each of them several strips of torn cloth. "We are going to place markers at each turn we take so it will be easy to backtrack if necessary. There may only be one way in and out of the maze."

Isa realized the wisdom of this plan and wondered whose idea it had been. Though she wished Edward would talk to her, would give her some sign of his feelings after last night, he was, of course, focused on navigating the maze and finding the tiara. Hopefully they would be able to spend more time together when they returned to the house.

Edward stopped and turned toward them. "Does everyone agree that we should seek out the center of the maze?"

Isa nodded and glanced at Louisa. "Yes. We'll simply have to hope that we come across any other clues during our journey to the center."

They walked along in silence, the overgrown vegetation towering over them and mostly blocking the sun. There were places where other foliage had linked the two lines of bushes, which would make it all the more difficult to identify the green cloak mentioned in the journal. All of them were on pins and needles, waiting for a clue to reveal itself. Isa studied the boxwood, looking for any sign that there had once been an opening in the dense bushes. Louisa slapped at an insect, and Isa rubbed her neck where a long branch had scratched her. Sweat ran between her shoulder blades.

Edward moved in front of them and attempted to hold back the large branches for them to pass by. They walked and walked and walked, and then Isa spotted the cloth that Edward had tied to their starting point. Her stomach sank. This could prove to be much more difficult than they had anticipated.

"We seem to have missed a turn somewhere." Thornbrook stated the obvious and wiped his face with his handkerchief.

"Let's go back around in the other direction," Edward said. "Louisa and Thornbrook, you study the inside of the path for an opening, and Isa and I will search the outside." He turned to the footman who was trailing behind them. "Branson, you can search whichever side you prefer, or both."

It wasn't until that moment that Isa considered the possibility that the maze might not move in on itself. What if what they were looking for wasn't in the center of the maze?

About ten minutes into their second loop, Isa stopped to examine the place where two bushes met. The branches appeared to be a bit shorter and less dense where they met in the middle. She pushed her hand through to the other side without much resistance.

"Edward," she called. He was ahead of her and hadn't noticed that she had stopped. "The branches here are thin." She attempted to stick her head through where her hand had been, but her bonnet caught in the branches and she had to untie it and take it off to free herself.

Once he had retraced his steps to find her, Edward untangled her bonnet and handed it back to her, then removed a small saw from his satchel and sawed through the two largest of the branches. After pulling the rest of them back, he said, "You're smaller. See if you can fit through and get a glimpse at the other side."

Isa forced herself through, wincing as she heard fabric tear. She only had so many gowns. She stepped into what might be another pathway. Boxwood lined both sides. "I think this is part of the maze, but there's no way to tell whether we're moving farther in or out."

"We'll have to take our chances." Edward pushed through behind her, bumping into her and then grabbing her shoulders to steady her. He tied another cloth to one of the branches while Thornbrook and Louisa pushed through to their side.

Edward charged forward and they followed him, stopping while he cut branches from their path and forged ahead again. This time it didn't take as long to find an opening. The edges of the branches barely touched, and they were able to slip through without difficulty.

They emerged onto yet another path. Edward smiled and brushed something from her cheek, his touch sending jolts of electricity through her. After a quick stop to drink some water, they continued on.

"Look." Louisa pointed to a series of openings that led to what looked like the middle of the maze. It turned out to not be much of a maze after all, as the openings were lined up in a row.

Edward rushed through, and the rest of them trailed behind. Isa stopped at the sight of a well standing in the center of the clearing.

"*Where the green cloak grows, light permeates the dark and deep*," She and Edward recited in unison. He reached for her and squeezed her hand.

Ivy grew along the sides of the well. Isa picked one of the leaves and twirled it in her fingers. "That has to be the green cloak." Excitement swelled within her. This was it. The tiara had to be here.

They stood there, glancing among one another, until Edward swung his satchel onto the ground and took out his flint and one of the scraps of cloth. Once he was able to light the bottom of it, he held it over the well, but it barely illuminated the top five or six feet of the brick-lined surface. He let go of it. Isa counted in her head, one, two, three, before there was a splash and the light went out.

"Did anybody see anything down there?" Isa asked.

They all shook their heads.

Louisa frowned. "What should we do now?"

Thornbrook spoke first. "Why don't we tie several of these together"—he waved one of the cloths they were using to mark the path — "and try to see farther down into the well."

Edward rummaged around in his satchel and pulled out a lantern. "Instead of igniting the cloth, let's knot it tightly and lower the lantern as far as we can."

"Based on the three seconds it took for the cloth to hit the water, that well is pretty deep. I'd say the water is at least one hundred feet down." It suddenly grew quiet, and the other three all turned to stare at Isa. "What? It's a simple formula to estimate velocity and distance."

The silence continued until Thornbrook pulled all of the cloth pieces from his pocket. Isa and Louisa added theirs to the growing pile, and he and Edward began tying them into a long rope. After pulling the end through the hook on the lantern, Edward wrapped the cloth around it several times then tied it securely to the rest of their makeshift cord.

"Let's all watch carefully for a sign of anything in the well. If the tiara is down there, it's probably wrapped inside something." With that, he began lowering the lantern. The brick lining the well was old and darkened with age and plant growth. It was difficult to see much of anything, to even make out the shape of the bricks.

As he continued lowering the lantern and they got closer to the end of the rope, Edward wrapped it around his hand several times and braced his knees against the outside of the well. The lantern swung slowly from the bottom of the rope, casting odd shadows on the bricks. They all scanned the sides of the well, hoping for a sign that something was down there.

Louisa sighed. "I can't see anything but the wall."

"Neither can I," Thornbrook said.

Isa nodded. "We need a longer rope."

Edward glanced at the sky, then turned to Isa. "You are correct, but we don't have enough time to make a trip back to the house before it gets dark."

Thornbrook wiped his hands on his breeches. "I could go now, by myself, and be back much more quickly than if we all went."

Edward shook his head. "I promised my parents we would stay together. They've already accused me of being irresponsible for taking the ladies into the woods without preparing properly first, so I don't want to add any fuel to that fire. Besides, we're expected at dinner tonight, so I suspect we should already be on our way back."

Isa blew out a frustrated breath. The tiara had to be down there. They were so close. "We'll just have to return tomorrow with a longer rope and the biggest lantern we can find." They all nodded in agreement with her.

Edward pulled the lantern up and doused the flame, then removed the cloth rope and stuffed it in his satchel. The lantern was still hot, so he carried it.

It had been another frustrating afternoon, and yet, Isa was still hopeful they would locate the tiara. After all, they had found the maze and the well. They had to be on the right track.

It was quicker going on the way back. They moved easily through the series of openings and followed the fabric they had tied to the boxwood to find their way out of the maze. It shouldn't be difficult for them to return tomorrow, when they would finally find the tiara.

"You are a horrible, ungrateful son, and I never should have shared the journal with you."

Anyone else probably would have been shocked at his mother's words, but he knew that she was just jealous that he was doing all of the searching while she had to stay to entertain the guests.

"Mother." Edward took her hand in his. "There wasn't time to tell you about what we found before dinner. In fact, the blame rests squarely with you. You were the one who insisted we be back on time. For all I know, we were moments away from finding the tiara, but we rushed back so we wouldn't be late for dinner." He kissed her forehead. "I promise to do a better job of keeping you informed."

"I'd prefer that you simply return with the tiara tomorrow."

They exchanged a smile. "I'll do my best."

Isa yawned, and Edward noted the dark smudges under her eyes. She had been unusually quiet. He would walk her to her bedchamber tonight, but nothing more than a chaste goodnight kiss would occur. He had kept her up late last night, and though he would like nothing more than to repeat their exploits tonight, she needed to rest.

"I'm going to the well with you in the morning."

Edward started to shake his head at his mother, but she was having none of it.

"I refuse to be left behind again. We've arranged to take the guests into Nunefield tomorrow afternoon, and Louisa is going to stay to help your father show everyone around the village. We're going to find the tiara tomorrow. I can feel it. We're so close."

She stood and kissed his cheek. "Goodnight, darling." She tilted her head at Isa, who was all but asleep, and pointed up. It seemed they were all going to make an early night of it. He wished he could carry her to her chamber, but there were still guests in the billiard room and the banqueting hall, and it wouldn't surprise him in the least to discover that some of his guests were in bedchambers to which they most certainly had not been assigned.

"Isa, come on. It's time for you to go to bed."

"Just give me another minute. I want to read through the journal one more time." Her head immediately dropped onto his shoulder even though she clutched the journal tightly in her lap.

"It's time to go upstairs." She lifted her head, and he stood up and removed the journal from her lap.

That got her attention. "Give it back. I told you I want to read through the journal again. There might be a clue I missed."

"You can look at it tomorrow. It's time for you to go to sleep now." He held his hand out to her, and she took it.

"As long as you join me."

He snapped his head around to check the corridor. "Shh. Someone might hear you." Had she over-imbibed at dinner? He didn't think so. Since no one else appeared to be about, he swung her into his arms and rushed up the staircase to her chamber with Biscuit on his heels. He would see her settled then go to his own room.

"I hate to disturb one of the maids at this time of night. Can you please unlace my gown and stays?" She turned her back to him before he could refuse her. She was a dangerous temptation. He did as she asked then turned away so she could disrobe and slip into bed. If he watched, it would be too difficult for him to walk away from her. All that smooth skin and those curves. He shook his head and focused his eyes on the door. As much as he wanted to spend the night with her, he wanted to ask her to be his wife more. He had to show her that he wanted all of her and not just a physical relationship.

"You needn't look away. I imagine I look much the same as yesterday." She hung up her gown and stays and turned back to him, clad only in the thin linen of her chemise, which left nothing to his imagination.

He gulped. The moonlight outlined every curve and turn of her, and he ached to touch her. He curled his hands into fists. "Yes, but tonight will not be a repeat of yesterday."

There were no sounds to be heard, almost as if she had stopped moving altogether. "You aren't going to stay with me tonight?" she asked in a small voice that sounded nothing like her usual confident tone. "Did I do something wrong last night?"

He strode over to her and took her hands in his. "Absolutely not. Believe me when I say that I would like nothing more than to stay with you tonight, but you are tired, and we've already cheated the fates by not having been caught together." There were other reasons, but he had difficulty remembering them in the face of her dejection.

She looked up and met his eyes. "Please stay with me. I need you to hold me, or I won't be able to sleep. Last night was the first time I've slept through the night since I left home to work for Lady Concord."

And that was it. He could not refuse her plea. He stripped down to his underclothes, then swept her into his arms and took her to the bed. She rolled onto her side and snuggled into him as if they already had a long-established routine. He closed his eyes, content to sink into the warm comfort of holding her tight. He was already drifting off to sleep when she started kissing his neck.

"Isa. You're supposed to be sleeping."

"I meant to, but you're so tempting." She kissed his neck and dipped her tongue into the hollow at the base of his throat. As if that wasn't enough to ignite a fire within him, she slid her hand down his chest and across his stomach muscles, causing them to twitch in response.

"Isa," he said again, half exasperated and already fully aroused.

She pulled away from him. "I'm sorry. It's just that we have limited time together, and I don't want to waste it sleeping. I want to spend as much time with you as possible before I have to leave. But if you don't want me…"

His heart clenched. "Isa, I always want you." He gently pulled her head up to him and kissed her deeply, then rolled her over in one swift movement. He grabbed the edge of her chemise and whipped it off over her head, then removed his drawers and plunged into her hot, impossibly wet core.

"My God, Isa. You feel so good." He wanted to stay buried inside her and never leave. She tightened around him, and he savored the moment before he started to move slowly in and out. "Look at me, Isa." She obliged, staring up at him with such trust. He stretched her arms up over her head so he could see all of her, and he watched her eyes widen as she came. He kept his pace, and she came again almost instantly. He let go of his iron control and joined her in release. Still linked together, he carefully rolled onto his side and kept her tight against him. He never wanted to let her go. Tomorrow he would talk to her about making their engagement real and hope like hell that she wanted it as much as he did.

Chapter Fifteen

Isa awoke with a start. Lightning flashed across the windows, and thunder boomed. Rain pelted the roof and hit the ground in sheets. It looked as if they would not be able to return to the well today. She rolled onto her back and studied Edward's sleeping form. He had stayed with her last night.

It was difficult to restrain herself. She wanted to touch him so badly, but if he could sleep through the onslaught outside, he must be exhausted, and she couldn't bear to wake him.

She was heartened by the fact that he had barely even questioned the incident with Thornbrook in the breakfast room. Surely he knew her well enough now to trust her, and would forgive her for deceiving him once she explained that she hadn't had a choice. His family was very close, so she felt certain that once he got over the initial surprise, he would understand that she had to do it to help George. Butterflies flitted through her stomach, and she promised herself she would tell him soon. As soon as the right moment presented itself.

She grabbed the journal that had somehow appeared on the table next to the bed and began rereading the second half.

He opened one eye. "Would you leave that blasted book alone already? We have all of the clues. We just need to do a more thorough search of the well, though it sounds as if we'll have to wait until tomorrow."

"I'm afraid so." Isa climbed off the bed and donned her dressing gown before pulling back the curtain to look outside. "There are huge puddles everywhere. Even if the rain stops, it's unlikely it will dry out enough for us to trudge through the woods."

The bed creaked, and Isa turned. Edward was pulling on his clothes as if he was about to be attacked by rabid wolves. She gulped. Clearly he didn't want to be here with her.

When he finished dressing, he strode over to her and pressed a quick kiss against her lips. "I need to get back to my chamber before someone notices I'm wearing yesterday's clothing. With it raining like that, no one will be outside, and I'm much more likely to be seen, and it will only get worse the longer I stay here. I'll see you at breakfast."

He clasped her hand in his warm fingers and kissed it, and then he was gone. She couldn't tell if he was rushing to get away from her or if he really was concerned about being caught leaving her bedchamber. With the rain outside, she had hoped he would stay longer and they could repeat their actions from last night, but that seemed to be the furthest thing from his mind. Perhaps she had done something wrong, or hadn't fulfilled his needs as he had hers. She sat on the bed and patted Biscuit. Maybe she had been wrong about his intentions. Maybe he didn't have any interest in marrying her. Maybe she didn't really know him at all.

B y late afternoon, the ground was completely saturated. Water pooled everywhere, and there was no sign of relief. It might even be too wet to go out tomorrow. Isa had taken refuge in her favorite room, the library. Though she had caught a few glimpses of Edward, they had not spoken since he had fled from her bedchamber that morning. She sighed and went back to rereading the journal, but so far she hadn't found anything new. It would seem that Edward was correct, and there was nothing else to be discovered.

She set the book down and moved to the shelves to look for something else to read. The duchess had invited her to join them in the parlor for charades, but she wasn't feeling very social.

"Good afternoon, Isabella. May I join you?" Lady Concord asked.

"Of course. Come, sit." She waved toward the settee. "I was just searching for something new to read."

"It seems as if I have barely seen you for the last few days."

Isa turned from the bookshelves and sat next to her. "I am sorry. I've abandoned you, haven't I?"

Lady Concord patted her arm. "Nonsense. Of course you want to spend time with your betrothed." She smoothed her skirt. "Her Grace has been very vocal in her praise of your sleuthing skills. I understand you have discovered the hiding place of the tiara."

"We believe so, but we have to wait for the rain to stop

before we can continue with our search."

"And everything is well between you and young Edward?"

"Yes, my lady."

She wrinkled her brow. "Then why are you hiding here in the library?"

Isa sighed. "It's been so long since I've moved in social circles of this sort."

"Isa, you were born into this world. You know how it works. Why are you hesitating?"

She glanced out the window. "I'm just not sure I fit into that world anymore."

Lady Concord took her hand. "Isa, have you told them your true identity?"

She shook her head, not meeting her employer's eyes.

Not only had she deceived the duke and duchess, Louisa, and Edward, but now she was lying to Lady Concord. She could not explain to Lady Concord that her engagement to Edward wasn't real or she would be betraying his trust. And since she and Edward had agreed only to a temporary arrangement while they searched for the tiara, there had been no reason to tell him her true identity. Now she feared she might have waited too long. If he wasn't able to forgive her for lying to him, she needed to leave. Soon. Her heart was already in peril, and she could not afford to risk her reputation as well.

"I thought not. What are you waiting for?"

"The right time to tell him."

"But don't you think he deserves to know who your father was? Who you are?" She leaned closer to Isa. "You have done nothing wrong. You are a victim of circumstances out of your control, and you behaved admirably in helping your brother. If you tell them, they will understand. The duchess comes from an unusual family, and the previous duke was a disgrace, so their family is not without its own scandals." She squeezed Isa's hand. "Tell them. They will understand."

"As usual, you are correct." She had no doubt that the duchess and Louisa wouldn't care about her true identity, but she wasn't so sure about Edward. Still, she had to tell him, and they needed to discuss their relationship. They had gone far beyond the bounds of their original agreement, and she had to know if he wanted to marry her. If he returned her love. If he could forgive her.

Lady Concord stood. "Come along, then. The duchess mentioned that they were about to start charades in the drawing room. I know she will appreciate our participation since she is having a devil of a time keeping everyone entertained in this downpour."

Isa clasped Lady Concord's arm and supported her as they went up one level to access the drawing room. Though it was a bit difficult to traverse, Isa loved the unconventional floor plan of Walsley.

They entered just as the duke stood and moved to the center of the room. Isa settled Lady Concord on a chair and found one of her own along the back wall where Biscuit could fit himself next to her.

"Eight of us go forth, but not back, to protect our king from a foe's attack," His Grace said.

So they were playing the old-fashioned version of charades, where instead of acting out a silent scene, they solved a riddle. Isa had reread Jane Austen's *Emma* the previous week, and they had played this version as well, where each person provided enigmatic clues, and the others had to guess the word they were describing.

"A spider's legs," Thornbrook called out, and everyone laughed.

"Who's the king of the spiders?" Someone called from the side of the room.

"There are eight sides to an octagon. That is all I can think of." Lady Phoebe shrugged.

"Pawns," Louisa said, pointing to the chess table next to her. She stood and gave her father a kiss on the cheek, then moved to the middle of the floor. For a moment, she simply stood there, biting her lip, then smiled and said, "If you have me, you want to share me, but if you share me, you no longer have me."

"Could you repeat that, please?" Lady Mary asked.

"If you have me, you want to share me, but if you share me, you no longer have me."

"I would never share you, Lady Louisa," Thornbrook called out, and several people laughed. Except for His Grace, who glowered at him.

Isa recognized his pensive look as he followed Louisa's every movement. He wasn't just flirting with her; he had feelings for her. Isa sympathized with him. She had been deliberately not looking at Edward since she had entered the room.

Lady Mary frowned. "A story?"

"No." Lady Phoebe grinned like a Cheshire cat. "A secret."

Isa shifted on her chair. She wondered how many of the others in the room had a secret. Probably most of them, but she was certain none of them were as big or as potentially disastrous as hers. She needed to speak with Edward. Today.

As soon as there was an opportunity for her to be alone with him, she would confess everything.

A footman carrying a tray of lemonade moved about the chamber. Isa took a glass just to have something to hold. The sound of chatter increased as the footman navigated his way around the room.

"Who does she think she is?" Isa glanced about her, but couldn't determine where the voice had come from. "She's no better than a common servant. I don't know how she managed to get Lord Kenworth to offer for her, but I'll bet you a hundred pounds he breaks their engagement by the time we leave Walsley."

After another glance around, Isa realized that the ceiling was domed, and the voices were carrying from the other side of the room where the mothers of several of the other ladies sat. Though she wasn't overly surprised by their opinion of her, it was disheartening for her to hear someone else voicing her worst fears.

Lady Phoebe stood and clapped her hands, then sauntered to the center of the room, ensuring that everyone was focused on her. She slowly licked her lips, then said, "What is always coming but never arrives?"

"Tomorrow," Edward said immediately. He stood and moved to the center of the room.

"You're so clever, my lord." Lady Phoebe frowned momentarily, then grasped Edward's upper arm and leaned in to whisper in his ear. The tips of his ears colored, and he laughed out loud. She walked slowly back to her seat, her hips swaying dramatically, then looked over her shoulder at him and blew him a kiss.

Isa froze in place. It seemed out of character for Edward

to encourage her promiscuous behavior, especially since no one else knew their engagement wasn't genuine, and Lady Phoebe's reputation was well-known. Perhaps he had been listening to the mothers and was beginning to doubt her as well.

Edward took the floor and stood there for several moments before speaking. "What will be broken if it isn't held?"

"A teacup?" Thornbrook tossed out. Edward shook his head.

Lady Phoebe jumped from her chair. "My heart."

"I'm afraid not."

She sat back down and pouted toward Edward.

"A promise," Isa said softly.

"Well done, Miss Winthrop," he said. Isa's stomach lurched, and nausea rose in her throat. She feared she might be sick, but a few deep breaths calmed her. She had made a promise to George, but she had also made a different sort of promise to Edward, and she had to tell him the truth. Now.

Her Grace stood up. "Miss Winthrop, I'm sorry to deny you your turn, but dinner will be served shortly. I promise we will finish the game after dinner."

"Of course, Your Grace. It is no matter." She stayed seated, waiting for everyone else to leave in the hope of having a few moments to speak with Edward. As expected, nearly everyone rushed out to go change for dinner.

The duchess waved for a footman to assist Lady Concord, who tilted her head toward Edward, reminding Isa of their earlier conversation.

When she was the last one left in the parlor, she stood and moved into the corridor. Edward was there, speaking with his mother, but as soon as Her Grace spotted Isa, she left.

He held out his arm. "May I escort you to your bed-chamber, Miss Winthrop?"

She linked her arm through his. "Somehow, that sounds rather inappropriate."

He raised his eyebrows. "Perhaps I meant it to."

"Shh. Someone will hear you." In truth, there was little chance of anyone overhearing them or even seeing Edward escort her, since there was a separate staircase that led to the family rooms.

"Isa, we're engaged to be married. I imagine everyone will understand." He glanced out the window that stood at the base of the staircase. "It seems to finally have stopped raining, thank goodness."

"At last. Though I imagine it will be another day or two before it will be dry enough for us to go back to explore the well."

He shrugged. "That depends on whether the sun decides to make an appearance. Of more concern right now is that it is nearly dark outside, which means we are in danger of being late for dinner."

They moved quickly down the corridor, and the closer they got to her bedchamber, the faster Isa's heart raced. Finally, they were there, and Edward opened the door for her. She would tell him now.

Isa clasped her hands, then twisted them before finally blurting out, "There is something I need to tell you. Will you come inside?"

He shifted his weight. "Can it wait until after dinner? There isn't much time for us to dress, and there will be many people moving about the house. I do not want to sully your reputation."

He was right. Though she wanted to get it over with, to finally know how he would react, it wasn't something that should be rushed, and they could not be late for dinner.

She nodded. "Yes, but I must speak with you tonight." He kissed her forehead, and she watched him rush off down the corridor. He had seemed a bit distracted, but perhaps it was just that he was as frustrated as she was about having to wait to find the tiara.

Isa shut the door and leaned against it. For better or worse, she would confess everything to Edward tonight.

With the help of his valet, Edward changed quickly and headed back downstairs. Isa had been somewhat distant during the day, and he feared that she had overheard the meddling mamas complaining about her during charades. He had wanted to call them out and give them the dressing down that they deserved, but their situation was already tenuous at best, so there was no reason to draw more attention to them. Isa was likely bothered by the same doubts that plagued him. Their original agreement had suited them both at first, but their relationship had grown and developed into something more, and he needed to know whether she also wanted to make their betrothal real.

He should have asked her, right then and there in the corridor outside her bedchamber. He cared for her deeply, and he wanted to marry her, and he didn't want to wait another moment to tell her, but with the gossip swirling among the guests, he couldn't take any chances with her reputation. It was going to be a long night.

He stopped at the threshold to the parlor. Lady Phoebe was the only one inside, and the cut of her gown was so low that he imagined he would be able to see her toes if he looked down while standing near her. She had been behaving inappropriately toward him all day, and he didn't wish to be alone with her.

There was a knock at the front door, and he backpedaled into the corridor while Phillips, their long-time butler, answered it.

"My lord, are you at home for Lord Stowe?"

Edward rushed to the door. "Stowey, is it really you?" He had been Edward's roommate at Eton, and though they hadn't seen each other in some time, he still considered him one of his closest friends. Edward had issued him an invitation to join the house party, but assumed Stowe hadn't been free to attend since he never responded. Stowe had spent the last several years trying to recover from his father's felonious investment scheme that had forced him to flee to the continent. When he died, Stowey had inherited an impoverished estate and a title that had a terrible reputation attached to it. He had finally had some financial success recently, and the memory of his father's actions had slowly faded as the members of the *ton* focused their attention on other scandals.

They shook hands. "I had given up on you."

He frowned. "I'm afraid I had a late start, and I've spent the last two days holed up at the inn at Nunefield, waiting for the Wye to stop overflowing its banks so I could get here."

Edward thumped him on the back. "You have excellent timing. We're just about to serve dinner."

Stowe's attention shifted to the staircase, and he took a step forward. "Isa?" A huge smile broke across his face, and he rushed to the stairs and engulfed her in an enthusiastic hug.

Edward's ears began to ring.

"What are you doing here? I'm sorry I haven't responded to your latest letters yet, but as you can see, I've been traveling, and they only just caught up with me in Nunefield."

His heart pounded so hard he could no longer hear what they were saying. If Isa was writing to Stowe, then they were much more than acquaintances. And they had an audience for this revelation since most of his guests were trapped on the staircase above them.

Stowe set her down, and her eyes immediately flew to Edward's. "It's all right, George," she said in a monotone voice. Her lips trembled. "I assumed your letters were waiting for me back at Concord House. H-how do you know Lord Kenworth?"

George's eyes narrowed. "We were roommates at Eton."

She nodded mechanically.

"Isa, what are you doing here?" he asked again.

"I came with Lady Concord. She is a long-time friend of Her Grace."

George closed his eyes for a moment. "Oh. Oh, no. I'm sorry, Isa. You're here as Miss Winthrop, and I've just cocked it up for you."

"Don't worry, Georgie. It's not your fault. I'm the one who is here under false pretenses."

Georgie? Here as Miss Winthrop? Who the hell was Isa?

A single tear slid down her check.

George took her hands. "Isa, it doesn't matter. You

can come home now. I've managed to make some sound investments and have paid off Father's debts."

Father. It hit him like a brick to the head. She wasn't involved with Stowe. She was his sister. Relief washed over him, and he nearly went to her, wanting to erase the disconnected look from her face. But once his brain engaged again, his anger returned in a white-hot rush. She had lied to him, and even after everything they had been through together, everything they had *done* together, she hadn't bothered to tell him who she really was.

His mother had been watching from the back corridor, but she finally found her voice and moved into the entrance hall. "Lord Stowe, it is lovely to have you. I'm afraid our dinner is growing cold. Perhaps we could all get better acquainted in the dining room?"

"Of course, Your Grace." Stowe bowed to her. "My apologies for arriving late and delaying your dinner."

She smiled, ever the duchess even in the face of turmoil. Edward lacked her skills of diplomacy. "Nonsense. There is no harm done."

A less true statement had never been uttered.

Mother led George into dinner, and Isa slid back against the wall, allowing the other guests to descend the staircase. Once they had all disappeared into the dining room, Edward gave Isa one last glare and exited out the front door.

Chapter Sixteen

Isa watched the door slam closed behind Edward. All she could think was *too late, too late, too late*. It was too late now. Everything was ruined with Edward because she hadn't had the nerve to speak out sooner.

Not knowing what else to do, she climbed the staircase and went to her bedchamber, where she began to pack her things. No doubt Lady Concord had already heard what had transpired. Isa knew she would be happy to have her stay on as her companion, but it was time to go home and do her best to make a life for herself. As herself. There would be no more pretending for her. Before she left, she would speak to the duchess about taking Biscuit with her.

As soon as she departed, the members of the house party would be free to gossip about her until a new scandal came along and she was forgotten. She would never be able to join society in London now that her duplicity had been revealed, but in time she might build a quiet life in the country with a gentleman who had no interest in the trappings of society. Hopefully her scandalous behavior would not hinder George's ability to find a suitable bride.

Once she had everything stowed in her trunk, she went down to the library to put the journal and the other books she had borrowed back in their places on the shelves. On the way back to her bedchamber, she borrowed some paper and a quill and ink so she could write notes to George and to Lady Concord.

She had just placed her last note on the table to dry when a soft knock sounded on the door. She moved slowly across the room, then allowed her hand to rest on the latch for a moment before she opened it.

Edward stood there. He cleared his throat. "They are playing whist in the parlor, so I don't think anyone will be heading for their bedchambers anytime soon." He waved a hand toward her bed. "May I come in?"

"Of course," she said and took a few steps back to let him through. She closed the door and took a deep breath before turning to face him. His expression was devoid of emotion and at that moment, she knew for certain that she had lost him forever.

She cast her eyes downward, unable to bear the censure in his eyes. "I am sorry about the manner in which you discovered my true identity. I tried to tell you earlier."

"Of course you did."

She lifted her eyes.

"You lied to me. You didn't trust me enough to tell me the truth."

"No, Edward, it's not that." She clasped her hands. "I couldn't betray George or Lady Concord."

He crossed his arms. "So you betrayed me instead."

She shook her head. "No, I waited so I could determine a way to sort everything out without having to betray anyone's trust."

"You failed."

"I know," she whispered. "If you give me another chance, I can explain."

His eyes flashed with anger, but he nodded. "All right. Be my guest. Explain this in a way that will make everything right between us."

"I did this for George. He could not afford to take care of me and repair the damage my father caused, so Lady Concord offered to take me in and pay me to serve as her companion. I decided to use my mother's maiden name to save Lady Concord from the gossip that would have surrounded me as the daughter of the infamous Lord Stowe. I hadn't come out yet, so it was easy enough for everyone to forget that Lord Stowe had a daughter. No one but George and Lady Concord knew who I really was. I never intended to hurt anyone. Especially you."

"Yes, well, you did. And it's much too late to change that."

"Edward, please. I love you."

His green eyes were as cold and smooth as emeralds.

"How do I know that isn't a lie, too? That every word you've ever said to me wasn't a lie?"

"I had no idea that you invited George here, or that you had been roommates at Eton." She lifted her chin and met his eyes, despite the tears rolling down her cheeks. "I was planning to tell you everything tonight. To confess and beg your forgiveness for the deception."

"Well, isn't that convenient timing. And yet, I am unmoved. Don't you think that was something you should have shared before you invited me into your bed?"

His words hurt more than if he had stabbed her with a knife.

This was it. It was too late. Their relationship could never be repaired. She blinked to dispel her tears and took deep breaths until she was calm and as devoid of emotion as he was.

"I plan to leave as soon as possible, so I want my payment."

His gaze narrowed, and she took a step back from him. Something flickered in his eyes, and then the light left them altogether and they were back to emerald stone.

"You'll have your money by morning. Then you can leave and never return." He turned and strode for the door, then looked back at her over his shoulder. "Unless you find that you are with child. Then you will return here and marry me. Not because I have any interest in you, but because I uphold my responsibilities. I will raise my child, should that be the consequence I am meant to bear for being foolish enough to trust you."

He shut the door softly behind him and, unable to continue to hold herself up any longer, Isa slid to the floor.

Edward lifted the brandy decanter and was surprised to see that it was empty. It had been full when he had entered his father's study earlier, and yet it hadn't been nearly enough to dull the ache of Isa's betrayal. The mantel clock struck two. Surely the guests had headed up to their rooms. Where were his parents?

He stumbled into the corridor and headed for the staircase. After missing the first step, he had to concentrate to place his foot on the stair. *Bloody stupid house with staircases everywhere.* It was damned inconvenient to have to negotiate a staircase every time you wanted to go to another room. He carefully moved his foot to the next step, then another and another, until he finally reached the floor where the library was. His parents had better be there, because he wasn't certain he could make it all the way to their bedchamber.

He pushed his way through the door, and thankfully his mother was there. "Edward. Where have you been? I was worried."

"First, I listened while Miss Winthrop..." No, that wasn't right. "While Lady Isabella lied to me, and then I went to Father's study and drank all of his brandy."

She touched her hand to his cheek. "Edward. You are in disarray."

"You would be, too, if the woman you thought you loved turned out to be a lying whore."

"Edward! Do not speak about Isabella in that manner." Mother led him over to the settee and pushed him down before taking the seat next to him. The faint scent of honeysuckle drifted to him. He couldn't escape her. Even in his own home she was still there, haunting him.

"You don't understand."

"What don't we understand?" Father asked. Edward hadn't noticed him before.

"That our engagement wasn't real," he said.

"What?" He wasn't sure which parent said that. They

were so close they were practically one person anyway. They were always together. Just as he had thought he would be with Isa.

"I offered to pay her to pretend to be my fiancée so you and the ladies at the house party would leave me alone. But then I fell in love with her and wanted her to marry me, but she's a liar, and I can't marry a liar."

All of a sudden, the angry face of his father was inches from him. "What did you just say?"

"I paid her to be my fiancée. Well, actually, I haven't paid her yet. I need to borrow a thousand pounds." He glanced around. His heart still hurt. "Is there any more brandy around here?"

"I'm going to kill him."

"Nick, calm down. We'll work this out."

He sensed movement, then Mother touched his cheek and turned his face toward her. "Edward. Why did you ask Isabella to pose as your fiancée?"

"Because it seemed like a good idea. And she needed the money. And then I loved her. But she lied to me. To all of us, so I can't marry her now. Unless she has my baby."

Mother's face dropped into her hands, then his father grabbed the front of his shirt and lifted him off the settee.

"Hey, what are you doing?"

"Give me a reason not to kill you."

"Nick, this isn't helping." She put her face in front of his. "Why did you do it, Edward?"

"Because I didn't want to get married, but then I did, and now I don't again." His father let go, and he flopped back onto the settee. The back of his head smashed into something, but he didn't mind since the pain distracted him from his aching heart.

Mother sat next to him. "Edward, Isabella did not set out to deceive you. She had already been posing as someone else for years before you met her. It's not her fault. You, on the other hand, set out to deliberately deceive us. So your father and I and Isabella are the injured parties in this, not you."

"Stop defending her," he shouted at his mother. He didn't want to talk about Isa anymore. It hurt too much.

All of a sudden, he was lifted off the settee again and thrown into the corridor. "Never speak to your mother like that again, or I assure you they will be your last words. I want you out of my house by noon tomorrow. I will give you the thousand pounds, but only because it is owed to Isabella. You will pay me back. You will find your own place to live and pay for it yourself, because I am no longer going to support you."

His father stepped over him and stormed up the staircase.

Then Mother came into the corridor. "You need to leave, Edward. I can't fix this for you. You'll have to fix it yourself."

And then she left, too.

Chapter Seventeen

Edward attempted to stretch, but his head was stuck at an angle against something hard. He opened his eyes, then closed them immediately. It was too bright. He opened one eye slightly and saw a closed door and a painting of his mother's dog that had traveled with her from the Bahamas. He was in the corridor outside the library.

He sat up abruptly, then leaned back against the wall until his head stopped spinning. Everything that happened the previous night came crashing back into his mind. He deserved the pounding pain and more. He had yelled at his mother and told Isa to leave. He had to figure out a way to fix everything. Mother was correct that Isa hadn't had any choice about deceiving him. She had been pretending to be someone else for a long time, and she had done it to help her brother, and not because she had deliberately set out to deceive him.

First things first. He needed to take a bath. He carefully

lifted himself to his feet and glanced at the clock in the library. It was only seven o'clock. He still had time.

Once he completed the harrowing trip to his bedchamber, he rang for his valet and ordered a bath. Then he found the toothpaste and brushed his teeth three times, hoping it would quell the brandy fumes. He bathed as quickly as possible and dressed even faster, then went down the corridor to Isa's chamber.

He knocked, but there was no answer. Not even a growl or yip from Biscuit. He didn't want to wake her, but he had to make sure she was all right. He pushed down on the latch and opened the door. The room was empty. She was gone. She hadn't even waited for the money.

He checked the wardrobe, just in case, but everything was gone. Biscuit was gone. Her books were gone. She was gone. The only sign that she had ever been there was the faint smell of honeysuckle, which he couldn't seem to avoid.

He dashed down the staircase, across the corridor to the opposite side, and up another staircase to reach Thornbrook's room.

He knocked, then knocked harder when there was no response.

"Go away."

"Thornbrook? Are you alone?"

"Kenworth?"

"Yes. Can I come in?"

There was a thump, then a curse, and Thornbrook opened the door. He was stark naked.

"I didn't expect to see you up and about this early after the…everything that happened last night."

"And I didn't expect to see so much of you."

He grinned.

"I need your help. Can you meet me in the stables in half an hour?"

"I'll try."

Next, Edward went in search of his mother, who, predictably, he found in the library.

"Mother, I'm sorry for everything I said to you last night." He leaned down and kissed her forehead. "I have a plan to win Isa back, but I need your help."

"Does your father know you're here?"

"I don't know, but I'm going to see him next."

She nodded. "What do you need from me?"

"Can you find out where Isa is?"

"Yes." She glanced away, and he got the feeling she already knew her whereabouts.

"Will you please tell me? I need to talk to her."

"Are you going to apologize to her and attempt to win her back, or do you just want to torture her some more?"

"I plan to apologize and pray that she'll take me back."

She smiled and touched his cheek. "Lord Stowe took her with him to the inn. It is early, so I suspect they are still there."

"Thank you." He kissed her cheek and rushed down to his father's study. After a deep, fortifying breath, he knocked on the door.

"Enter."

Edward pushed the door open.

Father stood as soon as he saw him. "What are you doing here? I distinctly remember disowning you last night."

"You did. But I wish to apologize first." He met his father's eyes. "I'm sorry I didn't tell you about the fake engagement. It didn't take long for me to realize it was a mistake, and I had planned to propose properly to Isa last night, but then George arrived and, well… I'm sorry. I didn't mean to cause a scene or ruin Mother's dinner party. And I never meant to be such a disappointment to you."

"Edward, you are not a disappointment to me."

"I'm not?"

Father shook his head. "I admit your actions are sometimes disappointing, but we all make mistakes. Even I have. The important thing is that you find a way to make up for them."

"I'm not sure that's possible. Why would she ever forgive me?"

He leaned against his desk. "Because it's obvious that she loves you."

"It is?" Edward wasn't so sure anymore. Father hadn't seen her after he had left her bedchamber last night.

"If you don't believe that, you're an even bigger blockhead than I thought."

Father was right. She did love him. She had said so. He just had to figure out a way to remind her of that. "I need your help. I don't know what to do, what to say, how to get her to even listen to me, but I have to get her back."

Father crossed his arms. "That's simple. You're going to have to grovel. A lot."

"You think that will work?"

"It worked with your mother."

"Somehow I cannot picture you groveling." He smiled at the thought.

Father laughed. "Trust me. I've had to grovel more than once. Just ask your mother."

So Edward wasn't the only one who had made a muddle of things, and perhaps his father hadn't always been as perfect as he seemed. Edward knew firsthand how good his parents' relationship was, so if even his father had to grovel every once in a while, maybe there was a chance Isa could forgive him.

"So what do we do?" he asked.

"You'll need to come up with some sort of gesture to show her that she can trust you."

"Such as?"

"Well, I gave the deed to Walsley Manor to your mother to convince her of the sincerity of my feelings."

Suddenly, Edward knew what he had to do, though he needed to speak to his mother first. Once their plan was in place, Edward went to the stables to finish the preparations. He examined the harnesses. This was the one part of the plan that he had not mentioned to his father. His parents would stop him if they knew what he intended to do.

"Can I help you, my lord?" asked James, their head groom.

"Perhaps. I need to find a harness that can be used to lower me down into a well."

"I beg your pardon, my lord?"

"You heard me just fine. I think something that I can step into, so my hips are supported, would be best."

"My lord, a harness is not made to hold weight."

"No, but it is made to pull the weight of a carriage or wagon, which can be quite heavy, so it ought to be able to hold me."

"Very well, sir." He walked down the line of harnesses and bridles until he found what he was looking for. "This is going to be uncomfortable for you, but if you don't agree with me, I am going to His Grace immediately to foil your plans."

"I didn't think you had it in you, James." Edward grinned at him. "So what are you suggesting?"

"In order to support your weight, at least two of the straps will need to fit between your legs."

Edward glared at him. "You do know that I am expected to produce an heir, don't you?"

James grinned back. "You'll just have to be careful. See here, you'll put your legs through here and here, where the horse's ears would normally go, and then we'll attach the carriage traces here to lower you down." He continued to share his plan with Edward, but he had tuned out. "You're coming with us. I don't trust anyone else to keep me safe."

"Yes, my lord."

Thornbrook ambled into the stables. "What are we doing?"

"We're going back to the maze, and you and as many grooms as James thinks we need are going to lower me into the well so we can either find the tiara or determine that it is not there." But Edward was certain it was there. It had to be. All the clues in the journal pointed to it, and he really needed to find it if he had any hope of winning Isa back.

"That doesn't sound wise," Thornbrook said.

"Exactly. That's why I invited you. If I die, they'll have someone to blame."

"Excellent."

"I have to go fetch Miss Winthrop…er…Lady Isabella. Will you stay and supervise the preparations?"

"What makes you think she'll come back with you?"

"I'll kidnap her if necessary, but I'm hoping the lure of finding the tiara will be enough to persuade her to return, even if I have to promise not to speak to her."

Thornbrook slapped him on the back. "Good luck, mate. You're going to need it."

Edward requested that his and his father's horses and the mare that Isa had used be saddled at once. As soon as Father arrived, they took off for the inn. He would do whatever it took to get her to forgive him. He leaped off his horse in front of the inn's stables and threw his reins and those of the mare toward a groom. A deep breath did nothing to calm him, so he deliberately slowed his steps and waited for Father to catch up with him. He could not rush into the inn and start making demands.

As soon as they entered, the innkeeper approached. "Your Grace, to what do I owe the pleasure of your visit?"

"I need to speak with one of your guests. Lord Stowe."

"Of course. Please, make yourself comfortable in the parlor and I will have Lord Stowe summoned."

"Thank you." Father settled himself into a chair that faced a window overlooking the street, and Edward paced across the room as he waited for his friend. He was certain Isa would refuse to see him, but he hoped Stowe could be convinced to help.

Stowe strode into the room and asked, "What are you doing here?"

"I need to see Isa."

He laughed. "Even if I were willing to allow that, which I'm not, she would never agree to see you."

Father stood. George noticed him for the first time and immediately bowed. "Your Grace, my apologies. I hadn't realized you were here."

"It is no matter."

"George, please," Edward said. "You know me. Despite my behavior last night, I love your sister and, even if she doesn't want to talk to me right now, she needs to come with me to find the tiara. She's been involved in the investigation all along. In fact, she is the one who figured out most of the clues, so she has to be there when we find it."

"I don't think she wants to be anywhere near you."

"Please, George. If you don't think she'll listen to me, then please persuade her to come."

"Who else will be there?" he asked.

"Father will escort us back to Walsley, and my sister and Thornbrook, as well as several footmen and grooms, will accompany us to the well where we believe the tiara is located."

George frowned, considering.

"I give you my word that I will return her safely to you."

George glanced at his father, then back to him. "Very well, if you can convince her to go with you, I will allow it."

Chapter Eighteen

Isa's stomach flip-flapped. She slowly descended the staircase and spotted Edward immediately. Her heart made a little jump, and treacherous hope rose within her. If anything, her feelings for him had grown stronger.

Whatever courage she had drummed up when she let George convince her to see Edward again quickly melted away. She hadn't expected him to seek her out and had hoped to already be on her way home.

Regardless of what he wanted to say to her, she knew in her heart that it was best for him if she left. Though George had made great strides in reestablishing his title and securing his properties, he could never completely erase the damage their father had done. Edward should not have to deal with the added burden of her notoriety, for surely it would never be completely forgotten. Especially after her duplicity had been revealed in front of the entire house party last night. They had probably already decried her for being as reprehensible as her father. Her resolve was set. It would be best for him and his wonderful family if she stayed away.

When she reached the bottom of the staircase, she stopped as if there were an invisible barrier. It hurt to even look at him. Her battered heart would never completely heal. Despite her resolution to resist him, there was a part of her that fervently hoped that she was with child. It would take the decision out of her hands, because she would not deny him his child.

"Courage, Isa," George whispered from behind her. "We've weathered far worse than this."

She nodded and strode into the parlor with her head held high, but faltered when she spotted the duke. Her shame burned inside her stomach. How foolish she had been to ever think she could be accepted into Edward's family after she lied about her identity and agreed to the pretend engagement.

"Your Grace." She curtsied to the duke, then nodded at Edward and waited for him to speak.

He simply stood there studying her until the duke not-so-subtly cleared his throat.

"Lady Isabella, we've arranged another expedition to search for the tiara, and I've come to ask you to please join us."

"My lord, I thank you for the invitation, but we've already made arrangements to begin our journey home."

He glanced out the window, then turned back to her. Then he clasped and unclasped his hands before saying, "Will you please come? You solved most of the clues and, well, I want you to be there when we find it. You deserve to be there."

He shifted his weight again. He was nervous. She had seen nearly every other mood from him over the past weeks, from excitement to anger, but this was the first time he had ever appeared unsure of himself. Her heart contracted, and it was all she could do to keep from touching him. She couldn't spend the day with him. She could barely keep from throwing her resolve to the wind and begging him to take her back now, so there was no chance that she could resist him for an entire day.

"Oh, I don't think—"

George exchanged a glance with Edward, then moved to her and squeezed her hand. "I think we can delay our departure for one more day."

Isa barely refrained from stomping on George's foot. It seemed that they were all against her.

"We are in agreement, then," the duke said and held out his arm to her. "Shall we?"

She could hardly refuse him, and of course she wanted to find the tiara, but she wasn't at all sure she could maintain her resolve if she had to spend the day with Edward.

Isa was careful not to look at Edward as they made their way toward the entrance to the maze.

"Do you think our markers are still in place after all that rain?" Lord Thornbrook asked.

"I certainly hope so." Edward and Thornbrook led their rather large party back to the well. Isa rode with Louisa just behind them, and an array of grooms followed with what seemed to be enough provisions to supply an army.

Edward stopped his horse when they reached the marker for the entrance to the maze. "We'll have to carry everything we need from here, and two of you need to stay and take care of the horses. I'll leave it to you, James, to sort out who does what."

He came to Isa to help her dismount, carefully lowering her while holding her at a distance from him. It was very different than the last time, when he had deliberately held her as close as possible so every bit of her slid over him. Her body craved his touch.

Louisa narrowed her eyes at Edward, took Isa's hand, and pulled her toward the first marker. They walked for several minutes in silence. It seemed that everyone could feel the tension between Edward and her, though perhaps they were just anticipating finally finding the tiara.

"So far so good," said Thornbrook, who was guiding their procession through the boxwood. He followed their markers until they reached the series of openings that led to the well.

They strode up to it, and Edward said, "This is it, James. You're going to lower me down in here, and you'll have to support my weight until I find what I'm looking for."

Isa broke out in a cold sweat. "No! That is much too dangerous. You cannot risk falling into the well." They would have no way to get him out. If he survived.

Everyone turned to her. She clasped her hands to hide their trembling. So much for not showing she still had feelings for Edward. She elbowed Louisa.

"Edward, Isa is correct. You are the heir. Father will kill you if you fall. Someone else should go."

"No." His steely voice left no room for argument. "This

is my quest, and I will see it through. Besides, it wouldn't be right to ask one of the grooms to do it."

"Thornbrook could do it," Louisa said.

"I could, but I don't want to."

Edward shook his head. "No. It has to be me."

James glanced down into the brick well. "Are you certain you're going to fit in there, my lord?"

"Yes, because I am confident that you can make it happen. Let's go."

While they made their preparations, Edward removed the lantern from his satchel and lit it.

"Are you sure you want to do this?" Thornbrook asked.

Edward glanced down into the dark well, as did Isa and Thornbrook. It seemed narrower now than it had before.

Edward nodded, and Isa's stomach contracted. "Edward, please. The tiara isn't worth your life."

He touched his gloved hand to her cheek and looked into her eyes. "I'll be fine."

She nodded stupidly, too afraid to touch him, and he walked away.

James strapped Edward into the harness and attached the carriage traces, then he climbed onto the edge of the well. "Everybody ready?"

They all nodded, but every face showed worry. For heaven's sake, there were seven men anchoring the harness. Surely that was enough to keep him safe. She hoped.

He climbed down into the well, but kept his hands on the rim.

"Edward?"

"Yes, Thornbrook?"

"I'll do my best not to drop you."

"Excellent." He removed his right hand from the side of the well and grabbed the lantern, then removed his other hand from the edge of the well. Isa held her breath, but the harness appeared to be strong enough to support his weight.

"Oh," he squeaked. "The harness is a little tight." Thornbrook laughed, and Louisa rolled her eyes.

"You can start lowering me now."

Edward held the lantern up and slowly swung it around so they could see all the way around the inside of the well.

He called up to them. "So far, there's nothing but bricks to see." They continued to lower him, but he remained silent. He was more than halfway down, and they were nearing the limit of their makeshift harness straps when he finally spoke. "Stop. There's a large cut out in the brick over here. It looks like it's been closed off with wood.

"Oh, well, go ahead and take your time studying it. It's not as if you're heavy or anything," Thornbrook called down.

"Hold tight. I'm going to have to swing myself to get closer to the opposite wall."

Isa moved even closer to the well, her heart thumping unevenly.

Edward stuck his legs out in front of him and pushed off from the right side of the wall. "I think there's a small crate shoved into a space in the wall. Is there any way you can brace the harness against the left side of the well? My left side," he added.

"Sure." The traces slowly slid to the left and Edward reached for the box, but he wasn't quite close enough. He pushed off the wall again to swing back, and the harness slipped. Isa gasped. Thornbrook braced his feet against the outside of the well and grunted as he tried to stop Edward's rapid descent.

The sound of Edward thumping into the wall was followed by a curse.

"I guess he's all right," Louisa said.

"Edward?" Isa yelled down into the well.

"I'm fine, but you're going to have to pull me back up so I can fetch the box."

"You should have listened to me," Isa snapped, terrified that he was hurt.

"I've got you," Thornbrook said, "but we're all getting tired up here."

"Oh, well, it's a veritable picnic down here."

"Let's get his lordship out of there," Thornbrook said to the other men. "Pull on my count. One, two, three."

Isa watched anxiously as Edward moved slowly toward them. "Stop," he yelled. "I think I can reach the box from here."

Edward pushed off from the opposite side again, then grabbed the edge of a brick and held himself to the wall long enough to grab the box.

Isa breathed an immense sigh of relief. "He has it. Hurry, pull him up now."

"Oh joy." Thornbrook said. "Remind me never to accept another of your invitations to a house party," he called down to Edward.

"Duly noted."

It seemed to take forever, but they finally lifted him up to the top of the well, and soon enough he was able to hand the box to Thornbrook and climb the rest of the way out. He dropped over the edge of the well and landed on his backside. Everyone else who had been holding him up took his cue and dropped to the ground. Once he caught his breath, he said, "You're all acting as if you just completed a difficult task. I'm the one who had to go down in there."

Apparently, they were too tired to respond to him. Isa was exhausted, and all she had done was watch. And worry. She ached to touch him, to make sure he was unhurt, but it was no longer her place to do so.

"All right, everybody gets the rest of the day off. Once we return to the stables, that is."

"How are you planning to thank me?" Thornbrook asked.

"Every day is a day off for you."

"Exactly. That's why I'm asking."

"Perhaps Louisa will kiss you to thank you for not killing her brother."

"No," Louisa said immediately. "I don't like you that much, Edward."

Edward laughed, but for a split second, Thornbrook looked crushed. Then he rallied. "You are an ungrateful lot. Perhaps Miss…Lady Isabella will reward me."

Edward popped up to a sitting position and glared at him. "What?"

Thornbrook grinned and held up his hands in surrender. "Never mind."

Isa glanced between them. For a moment, hope expanded in her chest, but surely Edward was not jealous over Thornbrook's teasing.

After one more glare at Thornbrook, Edward turned to James. "Are you done resting yet?"

He wiped his face with a handkerchief. "It's not so much the physical labor that wore us out. It was more the stress of knowing that His Grace would kill us if we dropped you."

Edward took the groom's hand to pull him up, then shook it. "Thank you, James. I couldn't have done this without you."

"If you don't mind me asking, what's in that box anyway, my lord?"

Edward glanced at the scrapes on his fingers. "I hope it is my great-great-grandmother's tiara. If not, it better be full of pirate treasure after everything we've gone through to find it."

"Well then, let's get you home so we can find out."

"Yes, we certainly can't open it here. Mother will kill us if we open it without her."

Edward's gaze met hers, and a flash of excitement shot through Isa. She couldn't help herself. She returned his grin. Now that Edward was safe, she couldn't wait for him to open that box. Finding the tiara was the best ending to her stay at Walsley Manor she could hope for.

Chapter Nineteen

When they returned to the house, Edward, for the second time that day, cleaned the scrapes and bruises on his hands as well as he could before making his way to the library.

His parents sat together on the settee, but the one person he needed to be there was absent.

"Where is Isa?"

His father smiled. "Don't worry. She'll be here shortly, along with Thornbrook and Louisa. Are you sure this is what you want to do?"

"Absolutely." He turned to his mother. "Are you certain?"

She nodded. "Darling, what did you do to your hands?" Mother grabbed his left hand and studied the cuts and scrapes.

He shrugged. "Nothing that won't heal."

James was hovering outside the door, holding the box they had retrieved from the well. Finally, footsteps sounded in the corridor and Isa, his sister, and Thornbrook appeared and sat opposite his parents.

Edward stood. "James, you can come in now." He nodded his thanks when James handed him the box, then waved him toward a chair. "With the help of Lord Thornbrook, James, and five other grooms, today we retrieved this box from inside the well that we found within an old, overgrown maze. It is my hope that great-great-grandmother's tiara is in here."

"How did you find the box?" Father asked.

Edward kept his eyes focused on the box. "We lowered a lantern into the well."

"Yes, you mentioned that before." He leveled his gaze at Edward. "But how did you retrieve it from the well?"

Louisa bounced in her seat. "For heaven's sake. Can we please just open the box? Edward had the grooms lower him into the well. You can yell at him later."

Father's face turned crimson, but Mother grabbed his arm to prevent him from erupting. "Edward, what were you thinking?" she asked, then shook her head. "We will discuss this later. Now open the blasted box."

Edward's stomach tightened. He lifted a hammer from the table and began prying off the lid. This was it. He wasn't sure they would ever recover from the disappointment if this turned out not to be the tiara, and despite the concern she expressed over his going into the well, he was even more worried that he would never be able to win Isa back without it.

The last nail gave, and Edward removed the lid. A polished mahogany box sat within. He removed it and set it on the table in front of his mother.

"Will you do the honors, please?"

She bit her lip and took a deep breath, then turned the latch and lifted out something wrapped in oilcloth. Mother unfolded the cloth and withdrew a velvet bag. And then she removed the tiara from the bag.

"Oh, my. It's even more beautiful than in the painting. Look at how the light plays over the diamonds," Isa said.

Edward studied Isa instead of the tiara. She had her lower lip trapped between her teeth, and he had to restrain himself from applying soothing kisses.

Louisa leaned closer. "It's magnificent."

"Well, thank goodness," Thornbrook said. "Imagine if, after all this time and effort, it turned out to be a rusty piece of junk."

Edward shook his head at Thornbrook, and Louisa elbowed him in the ribs.

Mother held the tiara out in front of her. She didn't say a word until Father leaned in and kissed her on the lips. "Oh, Edward. I can't believe you finally found it. After all these years."

Edward kneeled in front of her and studied the tiara. "It doesn't appear to have suffered any damage from being in the well for so long."

"I believe the metal work is solid gold," Mother said. "It's difficult to harm diamonds or gold."

Father strode to the door and wrenched it open. "Phillips," he bellowed. Moments later, the butler appeared at the door. He still moved quickly for a man his age.

"Yes, Your Grace?"

"We need champagne in here. Lots of champagne."

"Right away, Your Grace."

Phillips returned with the champagne, and once everyone had a flute, Father proposed a toast. "To Edward, for finding the tiara."

They all downed their champagne, then poured more. "To my beautiful wife, for never giving up on her dream of finding it."

They drank again, then refilled the glasses one more time.

Edward raised his glass for the last toast. "To Lady Isabella. We never would have found the tiara if it hadn't been for you."

Everyone cheered and emptied their glasses. Edward had never been more nervous in his life, but her worry for his safety while he was in the well gave him the courage to continue with the plan he and his father had orchestrated.

Edward lifted the tiara and carried it over to Isa. His hands trembled as he gently placed it on her head.

"Wh…what are you doing?"

"The tiara is yours."

"No." She shook her head. "I cannot accept it. It belongs to Her Grace."

"I'm sorry, dear," his mother said, "but we all agreed that you should have it."

She met Edward's eyes. "I thank you for the honor, my lord, but it belongs in your family."

Edward knelt before her, his heart racing. "I had hoped it might still stay in the family." He took her hands and rubbed the pads of his thumbs across her knuckles. "Isa, I know I behaved horribly to you last night, but I love you, and if you will agree to be my wife, I promise to spend the rest of my life making it up to you."

The room was completely silent, as if everyone had agreed to hold their breath until she responded.

She nodded, and Edward wasted no time kissing her. A cheer went up from the others in the room, and he remembered himself and reluctantly pulled away from her.

She raised a brow. "Did you give me the tiara just so I would feel obligated to marry you?"

"I might have if I had thought it would work, but no. I wanted you to have it no matter what." He swallowed, stalling before he asked her the most important question of all. "Is that why you said yes?"

She shook her head. "I would have said yes no matter what. Because I love you."

That was what he needed to hear. For the first time since everything went wrong yesterday, he could finally relax. Not caring what anyone else thought anymore, he leaned in to give Isa a proper kiss.

L ost as she was in Edward's scorching kiss, it took Isa a moment to sense that something had changed. She pulled back from him and belatedly realized that everyone else had left the room.

"When did everybody leave?" Edward asked.

Isa shook her head, pleased that they had left, since there was something she needed to say to him. "Yesterday wasn't entirely your fault. In fact, I shoulder most of the blame. I'm sorry I didn't find a way to tell you who I was sooner, but I was so afraid of losing you. I swear I was going to tell you last night, but then George arrived, and after I demanded you pay me to reveal the location of the painting and then agreed to take your money for posing as your fiancée, I figured there was no way you could ever trust me again."

"And yet, I do."

She bit back a grin, then glanced down and lifted one of

his hands. "What have you done? You'll have scars."

"It doesn't matter. Nothing matters as long as I have you with me."

"I have a salve that will help, but…oh. It's at the inn in Nunefield. I can bring it back tomorrow."

"No," he said rather loudly. "I don't want you to leave me again. I will send someone to the inn to bring your things back."

"Or I can ask George to move our belongings back here, if that's all right."

"Of course it is. I told you, I don't ever want you to leave me again." His eyes widened, and he jumped up and ran for the door. "I'll be right back. Don't go anywhere. There's something I need to get."

And then he was gone.

Isa busied herself searching for another book to read. They hadn't finished *The Count of Monte Cristo* yet, so maybe they could read it together. Or better yet, Edward could read it to her. She could listen to the deep, vibrating tones of his voice for hours.

Edward rushed back into the room, grabbed her hand, and towed her over to stand in front of the fireplace. Then he knelt in front of her and removed a box from his pocket before opening it and taking something out.

"I want you to have this as a symbol of my love." He slipped a gold ring set with pink diamonds on her finger.

"I know it's not the tiara, but since it's not very practical to wear every day, I thought you might like this smaller reminder of what brought us together."

"Oh, Edward. It's beautiful. And to tell you the truth, the tiara is quite heavy. This is perfect."

She pushed him back onto the settee and fell on top

of him. The tiara slid to the side, and he carefully lifted it from her head and set it on the table. The bristle on his neck tickled her lips as she kissed her way up to his mouth. "Did you forget to shave today?"

"No, but I may have missed a few spots. I downed an entire decanter of brandy last night, so I was still a bit drunk this morning."

"So you did miss me?"

"More than you'll ever know."

She leaned down to kiss him again, and after a few moments he tried to roll her over. "No. I think I'd like to stay on top this time."

"You would?"

"Umm-hmm."

"I'm not going to say no to that."

Isa giggled. "Your great-great-grandmother's descriptions in the diary were so vivid. I've been curious."

She grabbed his shoulders and pulled him toward her. He took the hint and sat up, and she slowly slid off his coat, running her hands over the muscles of his chest and arms before unbuttoning his shirt and pulling it over his head. When he tried to touch her, though, she slapped his hand.

"Not yet. It's my turn now."

He raised a brow. "It is?"

"Yes. You may only touch me when I say you can touch me." She slid slowly to the side and stood, then turned her back to him. "You may unlace my gown and stays."

He flew over to lock the door then loosened her gown almost immediately, but he took his time with her stays, untying them one at a time and pressing his warm lips against her chemise, which was an exercise in frustration and burning desire. His lips almost, but not quite, touching her skin aroused her more than she thought possible.

"My turn again."

"You're a cruel woman."

"Hmm. I wonder if there is something I can do to change your mind." Leaning close to his ear, she whispered, "Take off your pants."

He willingly obliged, and she pushed him back onto the settee, then lifted her skirts and straddled him.

"Have I mentioned that I love you?" he asked.

"You're welcome to keep saying it."

"So am I allowed to touch you now?"

"That depends. What did you have in mind?"

"Hmm. Perhaps something like this?" He slid a finger under the loosened bodice of her gown and chemise and stroked her nipple.

"Yes," she panted, then rubbed herself over his manhood. He squeezed her nipple and she pushed harder against him. Then he suddenly twisted his hips and somehow slid himself inside her.

She leaned over him and placed her hands on his chest, then began to move up and down the length of him. He groaned and closed his eyes, and she moved faster, adjusting slightly so he touched her most sensitive place. When he squeezed her nipple again, she exploded in sensation, and after a few more thrusts, he joined her in his release.

Drained of energy, she lowered herself onto his chest and snuggled her face against his neck. "I had no idea it could work that way until I came across that passage in the diary. I had planned to tease you until you couldn't stand it anymore, but you were too impatient."

"Why you little… Actually, you did a pretty good job of torturing me, but I have many more surprises in store for you. For example, we have yet to experiment in the tub."

"In the tub? We'll have to try that tomorrow. I'm too tired now."

"I'm sorry to tell you this, but we can't stay here all night. Especially not in our current state of undress."

"Do I really have to move again?"

"I'm afraid so. Unless you want my parents to find us like this."

She shot up so fast it probably looked like he had thrown her.

"Hurry, lace me back up."

"I believe I ought to put my pants on first." Which he did, then he helped her put herself back together before donning his shirt and coat.

"What do we do now? George will be expecting me to go back to the inn with him."

"No. I told you I want you here with me at Walsley. I'll speak with George and make the arrangements." He plunked himself down on the settee and pulled her onto his lap.

"I'll stay wherever you want me to as long as you're there."

"Speaking of where I'll be," he said, "how do you feel about Hampshire?"

"I've never been there. Why?"

"Kenworth Hall is just outside of Hampshire, near a charming little village. Since we're going to be married soon, and I imagine it would be a bit crowded and awkward for us to stay here, we should probably go visit. I expect we'll have a lot of work to do to make it habitable."

"Excellent. I should hate for us to be bored."

"That is something I am certain we will never be."

Epilogue

Isa rushed to hug her sister-in-law, whom she hadn't seen in months since she and Edward had just returned to town after enjoying an extended honeymoon in Hampshire. While they were in London, they had plans to order new furniture and fabric to have new draperies made for Kenworth Place.

"I thought you'd never arrive," Louisa scolded. "Mother is occupied with managing Father to make sure he does not interfere with the museum staff, and Thornbrook is late, as usual."

Isa raised a brow. "Who invited Thornbrook?"

"I did." She shrugged. "He's always wonderfully entertaining, which is just the sort of person we need at this type of stuffy affair."

"Have you two shared a kiss yet that was not the result

of a bet?"

Louisa shook her head. "Of course not. We're just friends. Acquaintances, really. Remember I wrote you about how I arranged for him to meet Lady Anne? He danced with her twice at the Richmond Ball and took her for a ride in his curricle."

"And that doesn't bother you, to see him showering his attention on another lady?"

"Of course not, Isa. I don't have any romantic feelings toward Thornbrook."

"More's the pity," Thornbrook said as he stopped next to them. "Lady Kenworth, you are looking positively radiant." He turned to her sister-in-law. "And Lady Louisa, you are as prickly as always, but I wouldn't have you any other way."

She rolled her eyes and earned a grin from him. "You won't be having me at all."

Isabella knew for certain that Thornbrook was pining over Louisa, and she was fairly certain that Louisa felt the same way about him, but she could not get her to admit it. Of course, it didn't help that both Louisa's parents and her brother refused to believe that there was anything between them.

Edward winked at her from across the room and joined her as soon as he was able to escape from Lady Phoebe. He kissed Isa's cheek, and thankfully refrained from touching her stomach, which he had been doing nearly nonstop since she had informed him that they were expecting their first child.

The moment it had been made public that the tiara was going to be on display in a new exhibit at the British Museum, they all had been bombarded by acquaintances who had written to request that the duke secure an invitation for them to attend the unveiling. The queen was supposed to make an appearance.

At long last, the museum curator waved to His Grace, which meant the presentation would begin soon. Edward took her arm, and they followed behind the duke and duchess, with Louisa and Thornbrook rounding out their party.

"Ladies and gentlemen, I give you the Duke of Boulstridge, who is going to share with us the story of a rather remarkable tiara that he has agreed to loan to the museum."

The duke glossed over the role of Her Grace's great-grandmother, who after all had received the tiara from a man who was not her husband, and instead focused on the efforts of his family to find the tiara, ending with Edward's daring plunge into the well.

It had required an inordinate amount of discussion before Her Grace and Isa were able to convince the men that displaying the tiara at the museum was a good idea. It was much too heavy to wear comfortably, and after having been hidden for so long, it seemed a shame to leave it to gather dust in a cabinet at Walsley. The queen and several other minor royals had also contributed to the exhibit, and Isa was looking forward to seeing the entire display. That was, if the curator would stop talking and open the doors so they could enter.

Isa rubbed her stomach, and Edward glanced at her nervously. If he didn't learn to relax, it was going to be a long six months or so until the baby arrived.

Finally the doors to the exhibit opened, and Louisa clasped her arm and dragged her toward the first display.

"This is a gorgeous piece," she said, pointing to an emerald necklace that had belonged to the Duchess of York.

They continued their path around the room, glancing at each of the displays. "Look at that diamond and ruby diadem." Louisa leaned in to get a closer look.

"If you say yes, I will give you jewels like that to make you feel like my queen." Louisa hurried off to the next display, and Isa tried to act as if she had not just overheard what Thornbrook had said. It certainly sounded like he had proposed to Louisa.

Edward waved to her, and she moved toward him to give them some privacy.

He tucked her against his side and they both looked at the tiara sparkling from its case. "Just think. If that tiara didn't exist, my mother and father would never have met, and we never would have married. In fact, I wouldn't have existed at all."

"That is a depressing thought, indeed." She squeezed his arm, unwilling to even contemplate what her life would be like without him.

Murmurs swept through the crowd, and soon they were hearing whispers that the queen had arrived. Never in her wildest dreams had Isa imaged that she might one day meet the queen. She reviewed the protocol in her head one more time.

"Darling, there's no need for you to be nervous about meeting her," Edward whispered in her ear. "If you can handle being related to my family, there's nothing you can't do."

Other Books By Ally Broadfield

How to Beguile a Duke

Just a Kiss

Acknowledgments

I am extremely grateful for my very forgiving family. I'm also grateful for cell phones—so they can call me when I lose track of time and forget to pick them up—and microwaves—so they can make their own food during deadlines.

My sincerest thanks to my editor, Robin Haseltine. We did it!

To the entire Entangled Publishing team for everything you do.

Rebecca Thomas, thank you for your friendship and for always being there to talk me down or administer a swift kick in the rear when I need it.

Last but never least, my sincerest thanks to my readers. The thought of you anxiously awaiting the next story keeps me going through the difficult parts.

About the Author

Ally has worked as a horse trainer, director of marketing and development, freelance proofreader, and a children's librarian, among other things. None of them were as awesome as writing romance novels (though the librarian gig came closest). She lives in Texas and is convinced her house is shrinking, possibly because she shares it with three kids, four dogs, a cat, a rabbit, and assorted reptiles. Oh, and her husband.

Ally likes to curse in Russian because very few people know what she's saying, and spends most of what would be her spare time letting dogs in and out of the house and shuttling kids around. She has many stories in her head looking for an opportunity to escape onto paper. She writes historical romance set in Regency England and Imperial Russia.

You can find Ally on her website, Facebook, and Twitter, though she makes no claims of using any of them properly. For information about contests and new releases, join her mailing list.